Praise for Jorrie Spencer's
The Strength of the Wolf

Rating: 5 Nymphs! "The Strength of the Wolf is the second book in the Strength series, but can easily be read as a stand alone as well. Ms. Spencer pours even more action and mystery into this intriguing paranormal romance..."

~ *Water Nymph, Literary Nymph Reviews*

Rating: 5 Roses "I like how she used the wolves' nature to hide from a traumatic event. Ms. Spencer again has skillfully joined wolf pack dynamics to human dynamics. This was truly a treasure to read and most definitely another keeper to my collection!"

~ *Robin S., My Book Cravings*

Rating: 5 Angels "You empathize with her characters' emotional turmoil, Veronica's amnesia and difficulty returning to humanity and David's attempts to protect his nephew and now Veronica. I totally enjoyed The Strength of the Pack and I can doubly recommend The Strength of the Wolf..."

~ *Dana P., Fallen Angel Reviews*

Rating: 4.5 Blue Ribbons "David Hardway is a marvelous hero. He is an honorable man with a huge heart. I fell in love with him in the first chapter when he rescued Veronica while in her wolf form. Veronica proves to be a strong heroine with a deeply caring nature even though she was physically and mentally scarred by some horrible event in the past."

~ *Robin Snodgrass, Romance Junkies*

"Don't miss THE STRENGTH OF THE WOLF. With a fine blend of romance, danger, tender emotion and multi-faceted characters, it's a sure winner."

~ *Lori Ann, Romance Reviews Today*

"Jorrie Spencer has created some wonderful characters. Their emotions were so vivid and realistic, I couldn't help be pulled into their lives."

~ *Stacey Brutger, Road to Romance*

B- "This book may not be for everyone because it is a quiet book, but it contains detailed characters who are both flawed with a compelling and a fresh new look at the werewolf mythology."

~ *Jane of Dear Author*

Look for these titles by
Jorrie Spencer

Now Available:

Haven
The Strength of the Pack

Coming Soon:

Puma

The Strength of
the Wolf

Jorrie Spencer

A SAMHAIN PUBLISHING, LTD. publication.

Samhain Publishing, Ltd.
577 Mulberry Street, Suite 1520
Macon, GA 31201
www.samhainpublishing.com

The Strength of the Wolf
Copyright © 2008 by Jorrie Spencer
Print ISBN: 978-1-59998-660-9
Digital ISBN: 1-59998-566-7

Editing by Sasha Knight
Cover by Dawn Seewer

First Samhain Publishing, Ltd. electronic publication: September 2007
First Samhain Publishing, Ltd. print publication: July 2008

Dedication

To D, and childhood memories.

Chapter One

It had been a mistake to be human yesterday, to sleep human in that barn. But after a long winter as wolf, she hadn't been able to resist. Now there were consequences—the dreams haunted her.

She wanted the dreams. They gave her a brother who named her Veronica.

She didn't want the dreams. Their violence disturbed her.

Had men always frightened her? She should know. But all she knew were wolf observations—the snow was beginning to melt and the days were longer—and wolf feelings. The she-wolf felt skittish this close to houses and cars.

She trotted, not allowing herself to dash in panic. Though the smells were wrong. Her nostrils quivered with gasoline and pollution, and even the distinctive musk of man. Her lip curled.

She moved forward. The smell turned abruptly to metal. Metal touched her paw and pain slammed down.

The bones crunched together. In her shock she yipped high, one time. Reflexively she pulled away, to no avail. She tried to make sense of the event. But it was happening again, this separation from her wolf's body, as if it weren't her own paw crushed between metal teeth, as if she were watching herself.

Her heart threw itself against her ribs and picked up speed, urging her to run. But when she pulled, the foot's ligaments tore.

Think! She froze, crouching, ignoring the fire in her foot. Despite everything she'd lost, she was a thinking being. The trapper would find and kill the wolf. There was nothing for it but to turn human.

And freeze to death.

With a will that threatened to break, she forced herself to look at the trap, to touch it with the other forepaw. Possibly she could shift to human and use her left hand to free the broken one. She closed her eyes and worked her way towards a shift. But it was too soon. The panic would not allow any kind of focus and her body, with the temperature falling below zero, resisted the change.

She heard whining. Her throat betrayed her with a noise she couldn't quite stop. To struggle all winter, to look forward to spring and the chance to be human again, and then to end like this. To stay wolf would get her killed.

It was dusk. No one, surely, would come till tomorrow. She had time to calm down, to concentrate on the change she must make.

Numb with pain and lack of circulation, her captured paw began to freeze. Her brain refused to focus on the shift. The whining didn't stop though she tried to close her throat.

Time, she repeated to herself, when she could think that clearly. Panic does not last forever.

Then she smelled man.

ℂ

Spring was late this year, which suited David Hardway just fine. He didn't always get to snowshoe in mid-March and he'd set out this morning for one last hurrah. Soon the snow would be gone and visitors—the human kind—would invade the park. He didn't consider himself a visitor, even if he lived and worked in southern Ontario. He'd grown up near Canoe Park and he allowed himself a proprietary sense of place.

He loved being here, even in drizzle, like the freezing kind that had just ended. Not that his snowshoes would be useful for much longer in these conditions. Good thing the truck was nearby. Just when he picked up speed, an animal cried out, high-pitched with pain. David stopped in his tracks. He waited to hear it again and perhaps locate it.

The park remained silent, except for the occasional car passing by. David turned and walked, straining to catch the sound of an animal in distress. The whining was so soft, it took a minute to register.

He listened carefully, then broke through the bush to make his way towards the creature. This wasn't a poor-me sound, this was an I-hurt-bad sound.

The whining stopped. As he came upon a narrow deer path, he saw a wolf jerk, trying to get away.

It couldn't. Its leg was caught in a trap. He moved closer. The trap was steel-jawed, not rubber-lined. This creature was doomed to death, not radio-collar and research. Or had been. He was going to change that. And report this to the park. *Goddamn traps.* He set aside his anger and focused on the quivering wolf.

"Hey," he called.

It whined. Its entire body cowered, ears flattened, while its lips pulled back into a snarl.

"That's right. Don't go down without a fight. The thing is,

11

I'm on your side."

He crouched, not close enough for it to bite, and it growled and snarled, showing its teeth.

"Good. You haven't been here too long if you're willing to fight, right?"

It shut off its threats, as if realizing they were futile. Its eyes pleaded with him.

"I bet that hurts like hell. Those damn things usually break the paw. Listen, I want you to get used to me for a minute while I figure out how I'm going to help you."

Its skinny body trembled. This past winter it hadn't prospered. Shoulders jutted and the coat was decidedly lackluster. Despite its large size, he thought it too delicate to be male, but maybe that was just starvation.

He swore, though softly, so as not to alarm the wolf. Her large gold eyes seemed to glow at him, and he stared back, waiting for her to break eye contact.

After a time, she did. He had to establish the upper hand, though that in itself would not free the wolf from the trap.

"These traps are illegal, you know. The park is supposed to protect you guys, not kill you."

She whined.

"That's right. I want to help. Let me free you before the trapper comes back with his shotgun. Or before that paw of yours is ruined. Your life isn't going to amount to much if you lose a paw."

He edged forward, still out of reach of those teeth. She didn't move. He opened his bag and took out his thick gloves. They wouldn't fully protect his hands from a wolf bite, but they'd help.

He pulled them on. "My name's David."

As he approached, she began to shake again.

"Easy." He braced for her to rush at him. Her whole body was vibrating. But she just stayed there, ears laid flat, crouched as low to the ground as possible.

Carefully, he placed his left snowshoe on top of her body. Not a lot of weight, but enough to prevent her from lunging at him.

She froze, whimpered.

"If you hurt me, I won't be able to help you, okay?"

She wouldn't look at him now, though her constant low whine wound through his nerves.

He talked, repeating himself, about friendship and help and trust, commiserating with her pain, making his voice a low, soothing vibration as he reached for the wolf's damaged paw, always aware that she could snap at him.

He examined the metal trap and found the release. His sister's boyfriend had demonstrated how they worked. In order not to further damage the paw, he moved as little as possible as he clipped the mechanism open and pulled the teeth apart. He eased her paw free and snapped the trap shut again so it wouldn't clamp onto another unsuspecting animal. Winter had been hard enough for the four-legged without traps to worry about.

Moving slowly and deliberately, he backed away, taking his weight off her, retracing his steps so he was a good five feet from her.

She didn't stir.

"If you were a dog, I'd take you into my sister's to fix that paw. Are you going to get up and return to your pack?"

She lay still and he walked around to see that her eyes were closed, as if she was unconscious.

Damn. Now she might freeze to death, if the trapper didn't come back and shoot her first. He wished his sister were here with a tranquilizer.

Once again he inched towards the wolf and after five minutes of ever increasing physical proximity, which included touching her pretty much all over, he concluded that she— definitely a she—was out cold.

Well, he might be an idiot to carry a wild, unsedated animal, but he couldn't leave her. He bent down, lifted her over his head and placed her on his shoulders so her legs hung down in front. With his heavy load, he trudged towards his truck. For a skinny wolf, she was big. In fact, now that he had a moment to think about it, her large frame and black fur were unlike the park wolves he'd seen.

"Where are you from, girl?" he murmured. "We're off to my sister's, in case you're wondering. Nell will look after you."

Nell was a vet and though she'd scold David for being a stranger, she had a soft heart. She'd help.

The trap, he'd report later. He hoped they nailed the bastard who'd set it.

℘

Veronica came to any number of times, though never with any great clarity. Mostly she was out, drugged, she recognized, with something attached to her good paw, something that didn't, thank God, hurt.

The lack of pain allowed her to relax, despite her fear of the cage. Well, lack of pain and lack of consciousness. She never stayed awake long enough to properly assess the situation. All she knew was the bed was warm and reassuring, the light soft, and the voices gentle. The man named David came and went.

The hands were respectful, and they handled her as little as possible. She appreciated that.

The impressions all blurred together until she finally woke. A real waking, where the world was clear, not smudged by odd, if comfortable, impressions. Impressions that did not engage her panic reflex.

Even now, she had an extraordinary sense of well-being and she suspected drugs were still at work. The paw's pain was a dull ache that her body had grown to accommodate.

"Hey, girl," said a nice voice, and she focused on a woman. To Veronica's disappointment, David was not around. She couldn't smell him.

"She's coming out." Veronica realized a phone was in the woman's hand. "Yep, she's looking at me. Seems alert. Now she's licking her paw."

It was shaven, where the intravenous had been attached, no doubt. How long had she been out? The other paw was in a cast. *Damn.*

"She doesn't like the cast."

Veronica glared at the woman.

"Well no, David, I wouldn't like it either. In fact, when I broke my arm I didn't have a heck of a lot of fun feeling awkward for weeks."

The woman looked at Veronica and spoke to her, tone reassuring, despite words meant for David. "My brother is obsessively concerned with your health so I'm to report every twitch in the next ten minutes. Apparently, I was insensitive when describing your reaction to your cast—"

"Okay, okay, Nell. Geez." Veronica heard David over the phone. "And I do appreciate you letting me know she's okay.

Anyway, stay away from her now. She's not to become Linc's pet. We want her back in the park, living her old life."

Veronica would have snorted if she were human. What a trip, her old life. Couldn't wait to return to what little she remembered of it.

Nell did snort. "Linc? Pet? He hasn't even come to see the wolf. It would cut into his computer time."

"You should disconnect the internet, Nell."

"Yeah?" Veronica could hear real anger now in Nell's voice. "Any other advice you'd care to dole out over the phone?"

"No."

The pause was rather long and Nell didn't seem inclined to speak.

"We don't want her to get used to humans," David added.

"Yeah." Nell rolled her eyes. "I actually remember that. Though what would I know about animals? I'm just a vet."

"You're the best."

Nell frowned. "She's not moving all that much."

"No?" David was all concern.

Veronica eased their minds by rising on all fours and limping around the cage which wasn't, she supposed, that small. But she still hated it.

"Don't worry, now she is."

"Good." David sounded relieved. "I'll be by this weekend."

"Great. I'll tell Linc. He'll be glad to see you."

Great, Veronica agreed. She wanted to see this David without the haze of pain and fear that had engulfed her hours or days ago. She suspected days.

David hadn't been large, she remembered, but solid. Fit. Blue-eyed with blond stubble. Not particularly handsome—did she used to go for handsome?—but she could like him. Well, she already did.

An idea took hold of her then, with great force—she wanted to meet David as human. Unlike earlier, her memory was reliable now—no longer fragmented, broken but coming together every day. Acting human, passing as human, seemed possible. Wolves were a little less demanding on the memory front but weren't inclined to have much to do with her.

Humans didn't recognize, as wolves did, that you weren't one of them. At least Veronica thought that the case. And if she wanted to do more than survive winters—which she'd barely managed this year—she needed to reenter human society, or make a friend. Given his actions, David seemed like a good candidate.

Maybe he wouldn't mind.

༄

She thought she wouldn't be frightened but the next day, as David approached, her heart sped up and her body quivered. She couldn't quite disentangle fear from anticipation. When he'd last been close she'd passed out, metal teeth clamped around her paw while her brain screamed *danger, danger.*

He crouched down at eye level and those blue eyes, sharp as the high summer sky, looked her over.

"Easy, girl. I won't stay. I just had to see you awake one time."

One time? thought Veronica anxiously, but then he smiled and she stopped shaking. He had such a nice, quiet smile and it was all for her.

"You're going to be okay, you know," he told her.

She limped towards him.

"No, no." He stood. "I won't do you any favors if you lose your fear of man. Look how that trap mangled your paw. Nell had to set bones and you lost half a toe."

Veronica felt alarm. Her *hand*.

"Hey, no worries. Nell assures me you won't limp. You just lost the bit above the last joint." He gave a quiet laugh. "Don't mind me. I like to describe everything, even when it can't be understood. Ask my students. If you're lucky, I'll explain Object Oriented Design Patterns to you sometime."

His voice caressed her. She came closer, put her nose to the chain links.

"You'll be out of here in a couple of weeks. I know, you want company, you're wired for it, but it's better if the company isn't human." He turned away and she protested. Her only friend was leaving and he didn't even know she would miss him.

He stopped, obviously torn, and she whined louder, pleading.

Again, he crouched down to look at her and her ears went back while she licked her lips. She would roll over if that would convince him to stay. He could show dominance for all she cared, as long as he didn't leave.

He shook his head. "You're beautiful. Gorgeous eyes. I bet you have a mate waiting for you somewhere."

She barked in negation, frustrated she couldn't communicate.

"No? Then you're a beta female, hardworking, a good aunt to all the pups. They'll need you."

She pressed her nose against the cage, wanting contact with him, and whined another greeting. *Be my friend.*

He stood abruptly and backed up. "You're breaking my heart here. If I were ignorant, I would adopt you. But I can't. You deserve a wolf's life."

But she wasn't a wolf. She just lived the life. Which was exactly her problem. This odd incursion into human company had wakened her need to be with people. And David knew nothing about what he'd done.

"Goodbye, Goldie."

With that he turned and left her for weeks. Nell occasionally sedated her so the cage didn't drive Veronica nuts. And the paw healed.

ᔕᑎ

The truck bounced over a deep pothole and David glanced back at the wolf. Goldie. Though he shouldn't humanize her. He didn't even like the name Goldie. It had slipped off his tongue when he was gazing into her startling yellow eyes and it had stuck. At least in his head.

"She's fine," Bob assured him.

David tried not to be irritated by his sister's boyfriend, and failed. "You know this how?"

"Wolves are resilient. I catch and release them all the time." Bob glanced over. "You don't believe me, but they're tough. The ones I collar aren't bothered by it. They have greater concerns—food, pack order, survival."

"She's been through enough," said David. "You cannot radio collar her."

"Wouldn't it be nice to know how she's doing? You obviously care."

David looked out the window without answering. He cared

19

and it would be nice to know. On the other hand, if she didn't thrive, he'd learn that, too. The collars signaled an animal's death.

"Come on, David. It will save the trapping of another wolf."

"She's been through enough," David repeated. "She doesn't need any more handling by any of us." He knew Bob's studies were important. They'd helped establish some anti-trapping laws. But he couldn't agree to saddle Goldie with that awkward collar when she already had a bum leg and sorrowful eyes, though the latter was not an observation he was willing to share with Bob.

Bob held up one hand. "All right. I had to ask one more time. Frankly, I'm curious. How did she end up in Canoe Park? She looks like a Rocky Mountain wolf and if she is, that's quite a ways to come. She must be a disperser. I'd like to see if she stays or goes home. She might have a tough road ahead."

David didn't want to hear that. He wanted her to have a pack nearby to welcome her home. Goldie had seemed a social creature, not one of those rare lone wolves. He'd visited her twice during her stay at Nell's and both times Goldie had recognized him.

The second time Nell had laughed. "Wow, David, this girl really likes you."

He didn't dare visit again. Besides, work had piled on, what with exams and conferences. He was off to New York next week and wouldn't be back here till July, for his annual canoe trip.

"Do you think the Calgary Flames will win the Stanley Cup this year?" asked Bob.

David picked up that thread of conversation. Bob liked to talk and the guy had been good enough to offer his expertise when it came to releasing Goldie safely. They needed an area well within the park area, yet with a sparse wolf population.

David's heart squeezed a little. He worried she wasn't strong enough to strike out on her own and he could almost talk himself into getting her collared so he'd know she was okay.

Wouldn't help her much though. Just rub her skin raw and get in the way. Wouldn't help her at all.

"David?" said Bob impatiently.

They'd been discussing who would likely be most valuable player. David threw himself into the conversation. Even if it was an uphill battle, it distracted him from worries about his wolf. He spent so much time alone with his research that he had to work hard to make light conversation.

Just when the effort became truly onerous, they reached the end of the narrow, rough road and Bob parked the truck.

David jumped out and rounded to the back, looking at Goldie, who panted, probably with fear. "Hey, girl, your ordeal is almost over." Even if life in the wild was uncertain, he was excited about her imminent freedom.

Bob walked around, let down the back door of the truck and jumped in.

Goldie snarled, ears back, teeth bared.

"Hold on." David held out an arm to stop Bob.

"David, it's fine, it's good if she doesn't like me. Come on, let's carry the cage off the truck."

David hesitated, then followed Bob on.

"Take it easy," Bob told Goldie. "I'm not going to hurt you. I'm going to release you."

Like the clever creature she was, Goldie stopped growling.

"Wolves like my voice," explained Bob, evidently pleased.

"Uh-huh." David reached for a good grip on the cage. Goldie whined a greeting and pressed her nose to the wires. She'd done

21

this often and he'd always resisted responding as she wished.

"She likes you even more," observed Bob.

Ignoring him, David took off his glove and put his palm against the cold nose. She licked him.

"Look at that." Bob was amused by the show of affection.

David wished Bob would shut up. David wondered, again, what his sister saw in Bob, who was making it impossible to say goodbye to Goldie.

"Wolves are intelligent," continued Bob, oblivious to David's irritation. "She must know you helped her."

Just as well he couldn't say goodbye, David decided, moved beyond reason by the wolf's show of affection. He put his gloves back on. Goldie didn't need his sentiment.

David reached for his end. "Ready?"

Bob lifted and, as they carried the cage off the truck, he said, "Well, you'll be passing by here in July, no? Once the black flies are gone? Then you can cruise through McKinley Lake and wave hello to her."

David grunted. They both knew she'd be long gone.

"I'll take that as a yes."

"That's right." David gave him a tight smile. "McKinley Lake in July. Come on, let's finish this."

Bob unlocked the cage and pulled up the side. They walked away.

Now Bob had the sense to be quiet. They watched while Goldie huddled in the corner, darting glances back and forth between them and the open door.

Then suddenly she was out of the cage and in motion, her long legs pushing against the spring ground, her beautiful body galloping away as quickly as possible. David was embarrassed by the rush of emotion he felt. She had her freedom. He would never see her again.

At least he'd allowed himself that brief moment of contact. Somehow, it seemed important.

Chapter Two

McKinley Lake in July. That information was seared into Veronica's brain. For the first few days after her release, she feared she would forget David, like she'd forgotten most of her life. But her memory remained stable. It accumulated. It just didn't go backwards beyond a few months.

She had to move forward, instead. Even if it was hard not to think of David all the time. He'd finally touched her, albeit briefly, and allowed her to taste him. It was with relief she realized she *couldn't* forget that contact. Her mind held onto the moment and refused to let it go.

July was still a couple of months away. But the time could be used to practice being human. She was rusty and needed to develop some minimal social skills if David was to be at all interested in her as Veronica, not Goldie.

She hoped to put on a bit of weight by July, too. Her breasts were more attractive when full and she had no illusions about what would attract a man to her. She was too strange to be a good friend and too out of practice to be a great conversationalist. If she ever had been.

Thoughts of acting human-normal made her nervous. She hoped David liked sex.

Veronica closed her eyes. She *knew* this wasn't how you courted another human, not when you liked them. But her options were limited, and attempts to remember social skills hit a blank wall. She wouldn't really know how she'd do in human company until she was there, reacting and responding by instinct.

But David was the right choice. At least she knew him. There'd been no mention of a wife or girlfriend. Nor had she smelled a woman on David. Like she'd smelled Nell on Bob, who had come by, trying to convince Nell that Veronica should be radio-collared.

Not that Veronica would have suffered. A quick shift to human and she could have taken off the collar. Still, she was inordinately touched that David had wanted to protect her. It was one of his kind acts she turned to for comfort at night as she fell asleep.

For the next few months, Veronica made McKinley Lake her home in Canoe Provincial Park—she'd learned of the park's official name during her stay at Nell's. Mostly she avoided wolves and people, except to steal clothing at a campsite.

She practiced talking. First on her own, to the trees and ubiquitous chipmunks, and later, with intrepid canoeists who were either braving the cool spring weather or the vicious black flies.

The men made her nervous so she kept things simple, like, *Hi! Miserable weather, eh?* They were surprised to see a lone woman walk past them on a portage. With concerned interest, one guy asked if she was alone and she pointed towards the lake and gave an airy, *No.* By the time he realized no one else was at the lake, Veronica had slipped into the forest.

As the black flies died down and July approached, Veronica kept a close eye—well, nose—on visitors, waiting to identify David. She wasn't yet comfortable enough to greet him as human. In fact, she wasn't sure *how* to go about it. So first contact would be as wolf and then, the next morning perhaps, as woman.

She hoped he liked women.

ℰ꙳

"Why don't you carry the other backpack?" David spoke as evenly as possible.

Linc slouched. His expression became even sulkier which David wouldn't have thought possible.

"That way," David continued as if he were talking to a fellow enthusiast, "we'll only have to walk the portage once, instead of twice."

With that little speech, David slung on the bigger backpack, then bent down to pick up the canoe. He flipped it up in one smooth movement.

"Get the paddles, too, would you?" he added once the canoe was balanced on his shoulders. Before he set off down the trail, Linc rolled his eyes.

David set his jaw. Linc was a problem. Not because he rolled his eyes, but because Nell no longer knew how to make her son listen. Bob was, of course, useless. So David had decided the boy needed to get away from the thrall of his computer. Two weeks of canoeing would break the spell and give Nell a reprieve.

Though it changed the nature of his usually solitary vacation. No problem, David told himself with what unfortunately felt like false heartiness. Even if he did spend too much time alone. At seventy he could embrace the life of a curmudgeonly hermit, but thirty was a bit young, especially when Linc needed an uncle.

Though Linc's steadfast refusal to buy into their vacation plans had led David to wonder if he'd have to tie Linc to the canoe until they were far into the interior of the park. In the end that hadn't proved necessary. Last week the boy had a surprising change of heart and declared he wanted to go. Not that his interest lasted beyond their arrival at the access point, when Linc realized he was required to paddle, too.

David wondered if his patience would last. He didn't have a long fuse. Linc had lost interest in the outdoors six years ago when he'd discovered real-time strategy games.

He's like you, claimed his mother, although David was a computer science professor, not a role-playing junkie. *No real friends except those avatars on Flamequest,* added Nell, smiling in worry. David didn't even know what Flamequest was, but it was true that he and Linc were both introverts who sometimes carried their isolation too far.

He just wished Linc looked bored. That would be normal and he could work with it. Instead, the boy acted as if his best friend had died this morning. The park's fresh beauty had done nothing to mitigate Linc's hangdog look. David figured it was going to be a long trip.

Well, if he continued to whine, he'd be as bad as Linc. David genuinely liked Linc. A sweet kid, even if he believed all adults had been put on this earth to serve him. Except for his father who ignored him. Linc's self-centeredness worried Nell and now she feared he was drinking. David hoped Nell was wrong about the alcohol. An immature sixteen-year-old, Linc's judgment was bad enough sober.

Linc had become more withdrawn over the past year. With two weeks of camping together, David hoped to draw him out. Or demand to know what the hell was wrong.

David carefully navigated the steep slope that descended to

the next lake and swung the canoe down at the water's edge. The portage had been short and not too uneven. He turned around and saw no sign of his nephew.

"Linc?" he called.

David sighed and took off his pack. It was their first day, they'd only just left McKinley Lake, and he had better see if Linc had tripped over a tree root, or something. God help him if the boy was sulking at the other end of the portage.

As he made his way back, he was pulled up short by a whine.

Damn. Someone had lost their dog. People shouldn't be so careless. Dogs died out here. He turned in the direction of the noise and his mouth fell open in shock. A wolf stood a few feet from him.

His wolf, the one he'd saved months ago. It had to be her, with the striking black fur and beautiful gold eyes. He'd expected Goldie to be long gone, and even if she'd decided to hang around McKinley Lake, a greeting like this astonished him.

She barked once, tale wagging, and her ears pointed forward as if he were her friend. Which he certainly was, but she shouldn't know it. You're a wolf, he wanted to say, a *wild* wolf.

"Goldie?" He had no doubt it was her, though she'd filled out.

She hesitated. Her entire body vibrated with anticipation.

"Hey!" shouted Linc, coming up behind him.

Goldie froze.

"Quiet," commanded David.

"It's a dog." Linc ignored him, his sullenness magically banished. "Hey, pup." He snapped his fingers.

David closed his hand over Linc's. "Stop that. It's a wolf."

Linc paused, unsure. "Really?" His face became eager again. "Cool!" He turned back to Goldie. "Hey, wolf."

"Jesus," swore David, then cut himself off when Goldie cowered at his tone.

"You're scaring it." Linc radiated disapproval. "What have you got against wolves?"

David grabbed Linc and pulled him back before he reached out to Goldie again. "Listen." *Idiot.* "I like wolves. I just don't think we should encourage her to make friends. She'll trot up to a hunter this fall and that will be the end of her."

Linc's face fell and David forgot to be irritated.

"This is the wolf I saved last spring," he explained to his nephew.

"Really?"

"Didn't you see her when she was at your mom's clinic?"

"No."

Perhaps wolves were more interesting when you didn't have a computer around.

Linc looked at Goldie who, to David's consternation, wagged her tail again.

"But she wants to make friends," Linc pointed out, puzzled.

Goldie took a tentative step forward, her whole body shaking with what might be joy, though David was more than a little nonplussed by the appearance of such an emotion. He must be making it up.

"She likes us!" Linc hadn't looked this happy for...years.

Nevertheless, David had Goldie's welfare to think about, too. "Look," he said sternly to the wolf.

Her ears went back and she stilled.

He let out a breath. He didn't have it in him to shout at her. Something about the eyes.

David rubbed his face. What was wrong with him?

Again, he braced himself to shoo her away.

"Uncle David." Linc put a hand on David's arm.

"Yeah?"

"What if it's too late? What if she's already friendly with humans?"

David opened his mouth to argue they nevertheless had to try, when Goldie took the plunge. She moved quickly and there she was beside him, nose against his palm, licking him, whining a friendly greeting.

"Aw, shit," swore David without force. She lay down and rolled over. "No, no, don't do that." But he gave up and bent to rub her head between his hands. God, she was a pretty thing, no longer starving, her fur glossy.

She was all over him, licking his face, her chest rumbling with happiness, and David felt incredibly odd. He'd thought his attachment one-sided and here was Goldie acting like she'd missed him terribly.

"Do you think I can pat her?" asked Linc.

Goldie stilled, as if she'd forgotten someone else was present.

"Try, but go slow." David backed up to give Linc access.

The boy carefully put out a hand and just touched her head before she ran off towards their canoe.

"She let me pat her." Linc smiled, pleased by the brief contact.

"Yup." David stared, dumbfounded, because Goldie now sat in their canoe, as if she were part of the family.

"Uncle David. I don't think this is a wild wolf. I think this is someone's pet."

She'd sure as hell acted wild in Nell's cage. At times, to keep her calm, Nell had sedated her.

Linc's face was alight with pleasure. "Can we keep her? Then this trip might be fun."

They walked down to the canoe and Goldie barked with enthusiasm. David found himself regarding her suspiciously. At which she started to grovel and lick his hand again.

"I really think," ventured Linc, "she's already lost her fear of humans."

David didn't see a way to argue the point. "Throw your pack in the canoe," he told Linc.

The boy grinned.

ॐ

She hadn't expected David to be with someone. Linc was a tall boy, taller than David, but young. Ungainly and skinny and not too strong. It was hard though, not to be charmed by Linc's enthusiasm for "Goldie". Especially when it was tempered by respect. He hadn't tried to pat her again. But he talked to her and he talked about her, all compliments.

Veronica wondered if David thought her pretty, too, then inwardly rolled her eyes. She didn't care if David found Goldie pretty as long as he thought *Veronica* was.

Which he would. Veronica was fairly certain she had attracted men in the past. Even the few she'd met on portages these past couple of months had shown some interest.

She had no home base, no money. She couldn't even meet David for coffee. So, she hoped to seduce him here. One of the most basic of human transactions. She hoped her instincts would kick in when it came to sex. Besides, she liked David.

Linc, however, threw a wrench in her plans, especially since he shared the tent with David. Much to the boy's displeasure.

"I thought there were two tents," Linc whined.

David's look was measured and not too sympathetic. "You're having enough trouble carrying your pack as it is."

"I could have brought a small tent."

"Yeah, well, you didn't. Just like you didn't bring your own food, so I'd advise you to eat what I give you or you'll be very hungry come morning."

Linc made a ridiculous face, as if he were going to choke on the gruel. Personally, she'd enjoyed it. Cooked food had been a welcome change, even for her wolf self.

"This sucks," said Linc. "Couldn't you have brought hamburgers?"

"It's summer. Meat doesn't stay fresh in this heat and I decided not to carry a fridge around with us."

"Ha, ha."

"You can grab a couple of pieces of jerky, if you want."

Instead, Linc grabbed his throat and gagged. David sighed.

Veronica was amused and it must have shown because David turned. "What are you laughing at, Goldie?"

His clear affection amazed her. She got up and went to him, letting him pat her again. He smelled so good, like sweaty man, with a whiff of wood smoke from the fire he'd lit.

"I wish she liked me." Linc held out his hand but Veronica couldn't bring herself to go to him, despite his rather forlorn expression. It wasn't that she was scared; he was too young and goodhearted. But a barrier would be crossed if Linc patted her.

Perhaps her wolf self had never liked being touched by humans, though obviously David was an important exception.

Linc cheered up as he pulled marshmallows out of the food bag and started munching his way through them. When they were half-gone, David said, "Enough. You're going to make yourself sick."

"No, I'm not," Linc scoffed.

"At the rate you're going, there won't be any left by the end of the trip."

"You only brought one bag?" Linc's utter disbelief was comical.

Veronica had the distinct impression David was counting in his head.

"I'll take that as a yes." Linc sounded put out.

"Yes." David stood abruptly, breathed in hard and announced, "I'm going for a short walk. Be right back."

Linc looked around uneasily. "Where are you going? There's nowhere to go."

David waited a beat. "I mean, I'm going for a swim." He added, with great self-control, "Would you like to come?"

"I'm too full. You're not swimming across the lake or something, are you?"

David frowned. "Why?"

"Bears might come."

David stared until Linc shifted.

"What?" asked Linc.

"Since when are you scared of bears? You're from here. You know what to do—get in the canoe."

Linc shrugged.

"You had better tell me what's bothering you sooner rather

than later, Linc."

"Nothing," Linc muttered.

"Uh-huh."

The silence stretched on.

"Later, eh?" Giving up, David stripped, then and there, to Veronica's shock and Linc's evident relief. The boy did not want to talk.

Against her will, Veronica's gaze swung back to David. She knew she had seen naked men before. She watched, unsettled by this one-sided intimacy. Her heart rate picked up, moving to a strange beat that mixed pleasure and uncertainty. He was quite beautiful naked—firmly muscular, solid, strong. She wanted to learn to love him as human. But she had yet to take the first step down that path and shift. She hoped he liked skinny and didn't care she was tall.

Stop being stupid, she told herself fiercely. If she wanted to seduce him, she had to strike up a friendship, not appear naked and throw herself at him. He was not that kind of guy.

David passed her by and she followed him. "Are you a swimmer?"

She barked.

"Good. Let's go."

But she stopped at the small, pebbled beach. It felt wrong to swim when he didn't know what she was. She was pretty sure that in her shadowy past she had kept her wolf world separate from the human world. Maybe with good reason, although right now all she felt was frustration. She wanted to be human with David.

This afternoon, she'd been too excited to do anything but greet him rapturously. After all, she hadn't been sure he would come to McKinley Lake. Vacation plans changed.

But he had arrived with Linc. The boy derailed her getting-to-know-David strategy, leaving her at a loss. She stared across the lake. David dipped below the surface and disappeared under water. Then he skimmed along the surface, swimming far away from her.

ᔓ

"We're losing the wolf." Linc spoke over the fire, through a mouth made gooey by the last of the marshmallows.

It was her second night with them and Veronica had no chance whatsoever to meet David alone. Despite his obvious reluctance to be on this trip, Linc didn't let David out of his sight. Which David chafed at, though the boy didn't notice. Linc wasn't observant, while she was keyed into David's every word and gesture.

"So it seems." David added a log to the fire.

"You don't even care."

"It's better this way."

What did David mean by that?

"Why'd she let you pet her yesterday and not today? I don't get it. Usually an animal becomes more friendly, not less so."

"I have no idea," admitted David.

Veronica knew. She wanted to be human with them but the transition seemed a little awkward if not downright impossible.

David turned to her and she quivered, retreating further. He sighed. "Some animals, like people, are neurotic. Maybe between the trap and whatever left her with a series of scars down the side of her ribs, Goldie has a screw or two loose."

Great. David thought she was a nutcase.

"You do care," Linc said triumphantly.

"I thought that was obvious."

"No. You didn't say so."

"I didn't say so."

Veronica's heart lifted. She was a nutcase, but one David cared about. That was all right. *She* didn't think she functioned at top capacity either. It didn't help that she could only bark and growl right now. Though wolves conveyed meaning and emotion with their range of sounds and body language, human speech was a more effective way to communicate.

She needed to shift. But first she had to steal another set of clothes. Taking David's or Linc's would not make a great first impression. And her original stolen clothes were back on McKinley Lake. They'd moved four lakes away from there. David was apparently doing a circuit, much to Linc's displeasure.

"Do you want to tell me what's going on at home?" asked David out of the blue.

Linc's head shot up. "What do you mean?"

"You know what I mean." This didn't exactly draw Linc out. Not that she *knew*, but Veronica couldn't help but feel Linc needed a little more coaxing.

"Nell isn't crazy about your new set of friends," continued David.

Linc looked glum. "I don't have any friends."

"Yeah? Where do you go Friday nights?"

"I don't have to tell you."

"That's what you say, rather rudely in my opinion, to your mother. Why don't you come up with a different answer for me."

The boy just glared. The conversation fascinated Veronica but she wished Linc didn't find it painful.

David held Linc's gaze until the boy blurted, "That's what this trip is about, isn't it? You figure after two weeks you can break me."

"*Break* you?" David's amusement made Linc glower.

Veronica had forgotten about teenaged boys and their over-the-top emotions. Then she started to tremble. *Where had that idea come from?* She didn't remember anything, certainly not teenagers. But the image of the slight, pretty boy of her dreams, enraged and shaken, haunted her. There was someone she had to protect. Her brother.

"Hey, Goldie," said David softly. "Why are you growling?"

Because I have a screw loose. She retreated further.

"No one's going to hurt you here," he told her soothingly.

"Hey, Goldie," called Linc. "It's okay."

It was not okay. Something had happened to her brother.

Linc turned to David. "She sat with us last night. Why not now?"

David shrugged. "She's wild and we can't help her."

"You can't help me, either," claimed Linc, darkly dramatic.

Between Goldie treating him like a dangerous wolf hunter and Linc accusing him of being the enemy sent to torture information out of him, David felt a little weary. "Try me."

To his surprise, Linc's words rushed out. "How do you know if someone's placed a hit on you?"

David blinked and thought how best to answer such a question. Linc had an overactive imagination, but surely he didn't have this kind of delusion of grandeur. "Placed a hit on you?"

Linc didn't answer.

"Tell me a bit more. It's not very common." David kept his tone as casual and inviting as he could manage.

"Yeah, I know." Linc tried and failed to sound offhand. "Just a stupid question."

"Where did the stupid question come from, Linc?"

"Nowhere. A movie I saw."

"Uh-huh. What happened to the kid in the movie?"

"He hacked into something he shouldn't have."

David could suddenly see there might be something serious here. Linc was stupid, but bright. Surely his long spells at the computer weren't due to hacking. Too obsessed by his games, Linc wouldn't spend precious time figuring out how to hack. Would he?

David groaned, fearing just that. "What kind of something?"

"A bank."

Shit. "Which bank?"

"The Federation Bank of Canada."

"Did you steal money?"

Again, Linc's head shot up. "No! I'm not a thief. I just believe in freedom of information."

"Oh? Freedom of information, eh?" David managed to keep from swearing at Linc. "What about privacy? Do you believe in privacy? Or, say, laws?"

Linc went back to glowering at the fire and David ground his teeth so he wouldn't tell Linc he was an idiot. This was a teenager with low self-esteem. A cliché, but that was Linc. Rejected by his father, except for once a year when the guy bothered to have Linc visit his second family and feel like a third wheel. And Nell, though God knows she tried, had lost the ability to connect with Linc. She didn't have the strength of will to fight him over his excessive computer time. Especially when it seemed to be the one thing that made Linc happy.

Surely no one wanted to literally kill Linc though. David decided to explore that aspect of this conversation.

"Privacy is important, too. I shouldn't have done it," Linc admitted, as if he were ten years old with his hand caught in the candy jar. He hung his head so low that David wanted to pull him up and tell him to sit straight and stop sulking.

"No, you shouldn't have." David's voice was more tense than he realized because Goldie began to growl again. "Easy, girl." He tried to project calm. After all, Linc had a history of lying. "You're not making this up, are you?" he said hopefully.

"No."

"I won't mind." David offered Linc a second chance to admit it.

"I only ever lie to Dad."

True. David's hope died. Besides, Linc was definitely frightened. "What you've done is against the law, Linc."

"Well, it's against the law to launder money, too," declared Linc.

"Uh, yeah." A terrible thought struck David. "Don't tell me you've been laundering money, too."

"Not me." A certain self-righteousness entered Linc's manner. "I don't steal. *They* have."

"They? Who?"

"The bank."

"The entire bank is laundering money."

"Not my dad. He doesn't know because he's too stupid to audit properly. But his boss is involved."

David dragged a hand over his face. "God, Linc, *Aaron's boss?* How long have you been hacking into the Federation

Bank?"

Linc poked at the fire.

"Linc?"

"Since my last visit to Dad's. Almost a year ago."

"Jesus Christ."

"I just wanted to see if I could do it."

David got up and started pacing. Goldie or no, he couldn't stay calm any longer. He breathed in hard, blew out a gust of air. Stopped and slashed the air with his open palm.

"I don't think, Linc, we can let this slide. This isn't a stay-between-us-guys type of thing. I'll have to talk to Nell."

"You'll talk to Mom?"

"Yes."

"Okay. She'll listen to you."

David heard relief in Linc's voice. That was good. Linc wanted his help.

"Uh, Linc." David came back to a point he hoped was irrelevant to the discussion. "What were you talking about earlier, when you mentioned a hit?"

Linc poked around the fire for a long time.

"*Linc.*"

"Someone from the bank found out I hacked."

"Why haven't you been arrested, then?"

"The police haven't traced my identity yet. I only hacked at an internet hotspot. That's why I bought a wireless last year. So they couldn't trace my ISP." He looked triumphant, as if David would applaud his cleverness, but David felt grimly dismayed and it showed.

Which gave Linc pause. "That's where I went on Fridays. And I used a pseudonym! Aragorn."

40

Aragorn. God, Linc was young. David sat down with a thump, trying to take it in. "So you weren't out drinking Friday nights." Alcohol suddenly seemed like a harmless way for a sixteen-year-old to let off steam.

"No." That Linc was insulted made David want to laugh. Or would have, in other circumstances.

"They'll trace the hotspot. And then you. It should take no time at all." They needed to get Linc into the police for a confession. The sooner the better. David hoped a confession would make them go easy on Linc.

"I stopped using that email address and I deleted everything."

"Okay."

"But before I did, I got an email."

"And what did the email say?" David prompted.

Linc looked up from the fire, his eyes hollow. He was scared again. "It said they knew Aragorn was Linc Berringer. It said I was a dead man unless I handed my computer over to them."

"Did you save the email?"

"To a file. Before I deleted it."

"Who wrote it?" David bit out the words.

"I don't know." His voice had gone high and young. David rose, thinking, *No one is going to touch a hair on this boy's head.* "A criminal."

"Well, fuck yes, a criminal. The good guys don't make death threats. What the hell have you done?"

"I'm sorry." Linc began to cry and David just stood there as if breathing was all he could accomplish.

While Linc sniffled, David pulled himself together, though his next words came out strangled. "Where is the computer now?"

Jorrie Spencer

Linc darted a look at his pack.

"You brought your laptop on the trip?"

He nodded and wiped his face.

David went over and gave the boy a one-armed hug, holding him until the trembling eased up.

"Sorry," repeated Linc, rather desperately.

"Okay, one apology is enough."

"I came on this trip so they wouldn't find me."

David allowed himself a wry smile which buoyed Linc slightly. "I wondered what convinced you to come along."

Linc swiped his face with his hand again. "What are we going to do?" The hope with which Linc regarded David made him feel like a fraud. A quick fix didn't seem likely. Nevertheless, David would get Linc out of this mess safely.

"Look, someone's playing games with you. If they wanted you hurt, you already would be, right?"

Linc didn't look reassured.

"But we'll figure something out. It will involve going to the police," David warned. "But if you've been threatened they'll be on your side." Or they better be. "For now, let me take a look at your laptop."

Linc scrambled over to his bag and dug it out of the bottom. "I bought a waterproof bag for it."

"Great." David wondered if their problem would be solved if the computer sank to the bottom of the lake. Probably not.

Linc unzipped the bag and plopped down beside David, his face eager, now that he got to explain how he'd hacked into the bank and what he'd found there.

Forty-five minutes later, Linc had convinced David this was trouble. He tried not to sound harsh. "Get to bed. I need to stay

42

up and think."

"You won't leave me alone?"

"Linc, when have I left you? I will look around the campsite for Goldie because my yelling upset her. But I'll stay within hearing range, okay?"

"Okay."

Linc rose and gathered his things for bed, slumping through his motions. David figured now was not the time to talk about good posture, though God knows he wished that was his biggest worry.

He could hope the email was sent by assholes who liked to scare the piss out of sixteen-year-old boys, but he wasn't going to depend on it.

Chapter Three

"So we're abandoning Goldie?" Linc asked David for the thousandth time.

"We are not 'abandoning' Goldie. Goldie left us, okay? She's a wild wolf with her own ideas." David tried not to sound testy. He'd found her last night and she'd even allowed him to pat her. But it had been as if Goldie was saying goodbye. This morning she was gone.

Linc's expression turned mulish. "I thought I'd take her home. I'd look after her and she could protect me."

"Linc," said David, exasperated. "She wouldn't even let you touch her."

"I did. Once." He hunched his shoulders. "I don't know why she let you pat her."

"Nor do I."

Linc looked back at the lake longingly. They'd packed up this morning after David announced they were breaking camp and going home. He hadn't referred to last night's conversation and now all Linc would talk about was that damned wolf. David hoped she was okay.

He slung on his backpack and reached for the canoe. From the corner of his eye, he saw someone walking down the portage trail. Hand on his pocketknife, he swung round to eye the stranger. He relaxed when she came into full view. A woman, and not a very strong-looking woman at that.

Not that David planned to attack every person he met on their way home. Even if someone was serious about hurting Linc, it was unlikely they'd follow him into Canoe Park.

"Hi." She didn't quite meet his gaze, which David found odd. Then she pushed her tangled mop of hair off her face to reveal a beautiful, if scruffy, woman. Under the circumstances, David had no desire to talk to a stranger.

"Hello." He turned to his canoe.

"Hi," she repeated and David looked back at her in surprise. But she was speaking to Linc now.

"Hi," replied Linc uncertainly.

"Where are you coming from?" she asked him.

Linc jabbed a thumb backwards but before he could elaborate David spoke. "From this lake to that lake. Like the portage sign says."

She smiled, without humor, and planted her feet on the ground as if she was not giving up on this conversation. Which was most inconvenient given David's current state of mind. He wanted to stay far away from strangers.

"Look," he said and she stared at him—a challenge or perhaps an expectation, he couldn't say. David's gut told him something was out of kilter. He wanted to get away from her.

Then she swallowed and he thought, *Shit*. Her stance was confident, shoulders back, hands on hips, but he feared she needed something from him.

To his annoyance, he noticed she wasn't wearing a bra under her T-shirt and it was cold enough to see nipples. He brought his gaze down. She also wore no shoes. Carried no baggage. He looked behind her.

"There's no one with me," she announced with false cheer.

David raised his eyebrows but what he felt was dread. She was an attractive woman who knew it; she might also be trouble. He had enough on his plate keeping Linc safe.

"I got dumped." She didn't look him in the eye. Though her skin was the kind of light brown that didn't blush easily, her face darkened with color. "I've been dumped before, but this is probably my worst-case scenario."

David looked at her in disbelief. "Someone left you here? Two days away from an access point?"

"Yes." Her expression invited him to join her in laughing at the situation, but David didn't think it funny at all. Nor did she. Even if she smiled easily enough. Too easily.

"So," she said.

He let the word carry. He wanted a full accounting before he committed to anything.

She shifted to glare at him, that expectation on her face again. "You're not exactly helping me out, buddy."

He wondered if he had some kind of strange radar that attracted people in need. "I'm not your buddy."

"I guess not," she muttered. "This is harder than I thought."

"We can't leave her here, Uncle David," put in Linc helpfully. "We're days away from civilization."

"That's what I thought, *David*." She sounded disappointed in him when she had no right to expect anything. "Or do I need to grovel and roll over before you'll help me out?"

"What the hell?" David said.

"I'm sorry." Her gaze jerked away and back at him again. This time he couldn't help but be struck by the color of her eyes. He'd never seen such a light shade of brown. Not washed out, but intense. "This is awkward, I know. I don't *like* asking for help. But never mind. I'll wait for the next people to arrive. Maybe they'll be more inclined."

David inwardly groaned. As if he could leave her here.

"Uncle David." Linc glared at him. "We can't abandon her, too. That's wrong."

"We did not abandon the wolf," ground out David.

She cocked her head and David thought she was going to ask about Goldie but, "So, will you help me?" was all she said.

Her hand reached up to rearrange her hair a third time and David didn't know if it was a nervous gesture or one calculated to make him notice her breast move.

She caught him watching and her smile became secretive.

Damn. Somehow David had more than his share of failed relationships where he didn't particularly like his lover. He knew why they happened. He liked sex more than intimacy. But he planned to stay away from this one, who spelled trouble. Even if she'd been left high and dry by some jerk.

Still, he gave up his hard-ass stance. "Yes, we'll help you."

"Good." She bounced on the balls of her feet, as if elated, and David felt something akin to alarm at her odd response. He didn't want a stranger around when he was responsible for his sixteen-year-old nephew. Who was looking at this woman with some delight. Not quite as delighted as he'd been with Goldie thankfully, but still.

She strode forward, extending her hand. "My name is Veronica."

He shook and her grip was firm though her entire body had the slightest of vibrations. He didn't like to label people as strange, but he was going to have to keep a good eye on Linc, no doubt about it. Thank God it should only take one more night to get out of the park and rid of her.

"I'm Linc." His nephew stepped forward, fresh and eager to make friends. Veronica shook his hand, too. Her smile seemed more genuine then.

She turned on her heel to address David. "Can I carry something?"

"We're fine. Besides, you have to watch those feet of yours. Don't tell me he—was it a he?—took your shoes, too?"

"Yes and yes." At that, she spun round and strode off ahead. Her jeans were loose and slid down to reveal a slim waist.

Goddammit. David wrenched his gaze away and turned to lift the canoe onto his shoulders. He picked his way through rocks and tree roots, making his way to the other side of the portage without misstep. He'd just have to treat the rest of their way home with equal care.

Between potential hitmen and stray women, this had to be the weirdest canoe trip he'd ever taken and he feared worse was to come.

Next year, he was definitely canoeing alone.

ℰ◌

Veronica walked quickly, lightheaded with not-quite-relief. She'd made first contact with David, and it had been rocky at best. He didn't like her, but he would help her. Their relationship could only improve from there. She hoped.

She also hoped she didn't hyperventilate. *Breathe, breathe, calm, calm.* If she fainted here, he might trip over her fallen body while carrying a canoe and then he'd be *really* annoyed with her. Instead of moderately so.

His antipathy dismayed her. After his reaction to Goldie, she'd somehow thought he would welcome her with open arms.

It didn't help that Linc had dropped his bombshell yesterday. David was rattled and worried about his nephew. She'd smelt his agitation last night. Well, if nothing else, she'd watch out for any dangerous men. Better than a human could, not that David would appreciate the help because he wasn't going to know what she was.

He'd looked her over not once but twice. Which pleased her, though his subsequent irritation was confusing. Maybe he was sexually frustrated. Not that they could do anything with Linc around.

Stop. Make friends with the man, and Linc, who no longer wanted to pat her head at least. Her thoughts skipped around, barely forming before they disappeared. Not quite panic, but in this state of mind she couldn't put her best foot forward. Unfortunate, given David's doubts about taking her on.

She suspected he helped everyone—wolves, nephews, abandoned women. Didn't mean this was the beginning of a friendship. Until her mind settled and she could say something to impress him, she would stay quiet and not make things worse between them.

∞

David would have been more annoyed with Veronica if she hadn't been so damned obliging all day. If Linc didn't want to paddle, she paddled, and was surprisingly muscular, given her skinny arms. If Linc didn't want to sit on the floor of the canoe, she sat on the floor of the canoe. If Linc was tired, she carried his pack.

Or would have. David had insisted Linc keep it. To Linc's

mind Veronica evidently fell into the adult camp of people who should serve him. One of David's worries subsided. Linc, immature Linc, was not trying to impress Veronica sexually. Nor did she play to him, like she did to David.

He wondered if she knew he had a hard-on when she leaned back in the canoe, arching her back and stretching, showing her breasts to their best advantage under a worn, thin T-shirt. He didn't wonder, actually. She knew and he disliked her for it. He didn't play games and he needed to make clear he wasn't interested. Especially under these circumstances.

If only she were one of those tall women who didn't bother with shorter men, though perhaps she didn't count the mere inch or so difference between them.

Twice Linc had started to tell Veronica about hitmen. Both times David had talked over him and Veronica, strangely lacking in curiosity, had acknowledged only the diversion.

David sighed. So the girl was polite. He didn't have to be paranoid about it.

Still, he pulled Linc to the side while Veronica, obligingly, gathered firewood. What a strange mix of Girl Scout and sex kitten. What a bad time to be distracted by a woman.

"Look, Linc, until we get this fiasco straightened out we do not, *do not*, I repeat, confide any details whatsoever to complete strangers. Do you understand?"

"Veronica? She's not a stranger now."

David clamped his teeth together so a stream of curses didn't escape. Why did Linc have to sound like a five-year-old who was confused about the concept of strangers? *I said hi, so he's not a stranger now, right?*

"Yes, she's a stranger." David held up his hand. "Don't argue. And don't talk to her about hacking. Talk about the wolf or anything else, but not that. Do you understand?"

Linc bobbed his head. "Okay. Geez, Uncle David, you're uptight."

"Yes. I am."

One advantage to having Veronica around—Linc showed some manners and didn't gag or choke on the supper. Interestingly, Veronica had a large appetite. She ate rapidly until she looked up to see she was outstripping both David and Linc. Suddenly self-conscious, she slowed down, to David's bemusement. He wouldn't have thought she cared, barefoot and tousle-haired, but to each their own.

David kept feeding her though. She was skinny and, since their trip had been cut short, they had plenty of extra bread and trail mix.

"Hungry girl," David couldn't help but say, though he should use tact or stay quiet.

Instead of getting a rise out of her, she looked abashed.

David found himself frowning and, for the first time, curious about her story. "How long were you on your own, Veronica?"

She wiped her mouth. "A couple of hours, that's all. My ex left at the crack of dawn. We didn't pack enough food though."

Idiots entered the park unprepared but, when it came to camping, Veronica didn't seem like an idiot. She could paddle, she could light fires and she could cook.

She didn't talk much. She communicated with those half-smiles when she caught him watching her, or she'd add a bounce to the swing of her hips or the sway of her breasts. All of which made David angry. And turned-on. Some women thought they could do anything as long as a man found them attractive. Except what Veronica seemed to do, since joining them, was help out.

As she collected the dirty dishes, her face intent on the mundane task, something turned over in his chest. She was trying very hard, he realized. He just wasn't sure at what and why. To please him? Did she fear he'd drop her like the last guy? Surely she didn't think she had to favor him with sex to make her way home. That idea made him a little sick.

She glanced up and caught him looking, though this time he wasn't just admiring some flaunted physical attribute. Her eyes pooled with emotion and he had the feeling he knew her from somewhere, yet her face was utterly unfamiliar. If beautiful. Her hopeful expression rattled him.

He turned away, uncomfortable. "Linc, get off your ass and help Veronica wash the dishes."

What was she hoping for? He looked again but she'd wiped the emotion clean.

"Just because someone asks for a ride doesn't mean you treat them like your servant," David told Linc.

Stung, Linc's face went red at David's scold. "I wasn't doing that."

David wished he'd put it more diplomatically. Though *pull your own weight* lectures inspired Linc to sulk, not pitch in.

"You were digesting your food," put in Veronica. "Right?"

"Yeah!" Linc glared at his uncle.

"Okay, okay." David held up his hands and Linc's angry blush subsided.

ᑌᑎ

Veronica decided she liked David better when she was a wolf. Although she couldn't decipher the look he'd given her while she was gathering up dishes. Puzzled? Less suspicious, too, which was a bit of a relief. But why?

She sighed. Her understanding of human cues was not great, even if she was aware of every moment David watched her. She didn't know if that was because she was half—the wolf half—in love with him, or because she'd enjoyed that kind of attention in a previous life. A butterfly wing of memory flapped furiously while her face burned. She'd been thought a slut by whoever had tried to slice her up. Her hand went to her left side, to the souvenirs along her ribs.

She didn't care if she was a slut, but she didn't want to be hurt because of it. Bile rose in her throat.

"Veronica?" Linc's voice came from far away. "Hey, are you all right? You look funny."

She wrenched her mind out of the indecipherable noise. Loud and incomprehensible, it was all her memory ever offered her of the past. Standing up, she swayed.

"I'm good," she lied. "The dishes are done." She walked up to the campsite and let the cooling night air take some of the heat off her face.

As they returned, David was watching her again, but more as a puzzle than a sex object. She felt her shoulders sag. She didn't want him to figure her out. That would be disastrous. Sex object first, and then affection. She thought it a good strategy. It even seemed familiar. And there sure wasn't a budding friendship developing here. Tomorrow they would part and David had zero interest in seeing her again.

"Where's Veronica going to sleep?" asked Linc.

"Don't worry about me." She hoped it wasn't obvious she wanted to sleep with David. Embarrassing how badly she wanted the physical contact. That handshake at the first meet had shocked her with its skin-on-skin contact. All day, she had visited and revisited that moment.

Get a grip.

David held out a sleeping bag and roll to her. "You can have these tonight. It won't rain."

She stared. "They're yours."

He gave the smallest of shrugs, intent on the gift of bedding.

The gesture touched her. Maybe her human half could love David, too. She didn't care if it was reciprocated as long as he thought her half-decent company. He wouldn't even have to *know.*

"But what will you sleep on?" She didn't want to put him out. Besides, she was used to hard ground.

"Stuff. Don't worry about it." He thrust the sleeping gear at her.

"Thanks," she said.

Linc strolled off to take care of business and Veronica was alone with David. She couldn't stop herself from licking her lips suggestively. "I'll take that spot behind the bushes. But don't visit me at night. I sleep nude."

"Good for you," he drawled.

"You don't like me much, do you?" She was proud to keep her voice free from any kind of tremor. She had so little time, no experience to draw upon and David was not making it easy.

"I don't know you."

"You could." Her heart rate kicked up as she waited for his answer.

Their shared gaze lengthened and David's eyes, to Veronica's relief, darkened with desire.

"Do you usually work this quickly?" That wasn't admiration in his voice.

54

She tried for a nonchalant shrug to accompany her truth. "I don't know."

"Linc's here and I'm looking after my nephew, okay?" *Back off*, he was saying.

"Sure. I was thinking later, to tell you the truth. After the trip. Maybe we could meet up."

"Why would I do that?" He sounded fed up or perhaps baffled by her attempt to connect. She couldn't read him.

Still, it hurt, so she smiled. Her stupid smile. Like she was an idiot smile.

"You don't know me," he added, to soften the blow.

"I could." Before he rejected her again, she stalked off with his sleeping gear. She'd have the smell of him tonight, if not the man himself.

That she heard his breath bail out, offered her some satisfaction.

ဆ

David lay on his back, eyes wide open in the blackness of the tent. After Linc's confession last night, he hadn't slept. But at least he'd been able to wander around the campsite and sit by the lake, listening to the water lap at the shore.

Tonight, if he went out he'd run into Veronica who slept nude. Not that he lacked self-discipline, but he didn't feel like blatantly rejecting an overture. Again. And he had to admit the temptation was there. Right now he would welcome a certain kind of mindless oblivion.

But, *no*. He'd ruled out hit and runs a couple of years ago. Besides, he was stuck canoeing with her tomorrow. How awkward would that be? Especially with Linc around.

Linc. He shook his head. The real problem—he was wired and worried sick about Linc.

Hitmen. God knows he hoped that email to Linc had been a crank. But it wasn't only that—Linc had broken a rather serious law. Nell had enough on her plate, running her business, working hard on her one-sided relationship with Bob and looking after Mom's emotional needs.

Guilt struck again. He and Mom had fallen out years ago. After some reconciliation, their relationship remained strained and they didn't really talk. Certainly not like Mom's tearful midnight conversations with Nell that David couldn't stomach anyway.

Water splashed and David jerked up to sitting. The sound came again. Maybe from the loon whose lonely call had echoed about the lake earlier. But under the circumstances, he had to check it out. He reached for the tent's door.

Against the silence of the park's night, the zipper sounded loud in David's ears. He looked at Linc who slept like a log. He shut the tent back up.

Dressed only in boxers, a flashlight in one hand and a pocketknife in the other, he walked down to the shore, his bare feet on dirt and pine needles, and then on rock that rose up out of the water. He came to its edge and crouched down.

He wasn't surprised or even dismayed—though he should have been—to see Veronica swim breaststroke towards him, her hair sleek and dark with water. He thought of otters.

"Hi," she greeted him.

He nodded in acknowledgment and put his flashlight down on the rock so it didn't blind her.

She reached the rocky ledge below him and hooked her arms on it. Then looked up at him with enormous eyes and bare shoulders. He couldn't make out anything else.

He glanced back at the tent.

"The water's warm," she said and his gaze came back to rest on hers, golden in the night. "Come on in."

If she'd smiled, he would have turned away and left. But her face was quiet, watchful.

"You don't," he stopped and cleared his throat. "This isn't necessary."

"Necessary?" She sounded puzzled.

"You don't think you have to trade for a ride home, do you?"

She shook her head mutely and he didn't know what to say.

"I like you, David." The words were soft, an admission.

He was embarrassed. He hadn't been nice. Nor did he like her, although he admired her industry. And her body.

He switched off the flashlight. "I'm not coming in, Veronica."

"Okay." She climbed out. Her body was gray against the blackness of the night and difficult to see clearly. His breath hitched.

He stood abruptly. "Look," he said with little force, and couldn't even continue that rebuff when she shivered beside him.

He no longer wanted to say no. As his blood pooled south, he tried to remember why it was important not to have sex with someone who was willing.

She stepped up beside him and reached out to clasp his hand. Her cool fingers found his wrapped around the pocketknife and she stiffened.

"A knife?" she asked as he transferred it to the other hand.

"I'm a protective uncle." A rattled uncle, he wanted to explain, but he would not give her details of the Linc debacle. So he let himself sound stupid, expecting her to laugh at him.

She just stood still, as if at a loss. "Someone used a knife on me once. Here." She took his hand and skimmed it down her side. He felt where skin was rough then smooth then rough. "I don't know why."

Aw, shit. He didn't know what to say so he held fast to her fingers, squeezing them gently as if that would reassure her.

Neither of them looked at each other.

"I shouldn't have said that. Wrong time and place, right?" The question seemed genuine and it struck him that she was oddly brave, putting herself out here like this. He should let go of her hand and return to the tent, but he couldn't release her now. Not without saying *something*.

"Was it a boyfriend?"

She hesitated. "Yes." She sounded unsure.

"I think you'd better find a better quality of boyfriend, Veronica."

"Yes. I'm going to try." Her earnest tone made him feel helpless.

"Good."

She smiled in the grayness. "You're nice, David. I'll show you where I put your sleeping bag, okay?"

He went, unable to think beyond her past violence, her delicate hand in his and his erection. Unable, really, to say no.

When they reached the sleeping bag, she released him, placed two palms on his hips, and slid her hands down, taking his boxers with them.

He woke up, then, to what was happening. This was not some stupid daydream. He was not sleepwalking. He pulled her up to face him.

"What?" Her confusion made his next words die in his mouth. Instead of saying, *look*, not that he'd thought beyond that one word, he curled a hand around the nape of her beautiful neck and kissed her.

Good, he thought rather furiously and his kiss intensified. As her mouth softened, he skimmed his hand down her smooth side, still slick with lake water, and cupped her bottom.

Her entire body tensed up.

He broke the kiss. "Veronica?"

Ignoring his question, she clasped his hands and pulled him down so she was on top. *Okay.* Distracted by her intent, eager touch, he wished he could read her better, but she was rubbing the head of his slick cock with her thumb and he couldn't think.

Couldn't think but to remember the kiss had surprised her and he eased her towards him, looking at her this time, before their mouths met. The kiss started sweet and became intense. He slid fingers over a lovely full breast and delightful nipple. Her noises were pleased and high. Then he reached lower, towards her sex, slowly, slowly. He wanted to see if she was ready for him, but she stiffened again.

Okay.

He didn't understand why she'd initiated this when she wasn't able to relax, but he thought he could do something about it, if she let him.

"Veronica."

"Now," she whispered urgently, shifting so she was against him, apparently ready for intercourse. Well, maybe that would relax her and his body agreed.

Condom, his brain managed to think, and he uttered the

word.

"I've got that covered," she said nonsensically.

He wrapped both arms around her to still her. "You're not ready. And I'm *too* ready."

"I am ready. *Please.*" She broke free of his embrace and sat up as she simultaneously moved down on him. His cock pushed through to greet her and she moved and he could no longer think.

Three strokes and pleasure banked. He was pulsing.

It felt good, sex usually did, and he tried to stay in the moment, even if it had arrived too soon. She was above him, her hands pinned his upper arms, though he could have moved any time he wanted. Something was wrong.

She was shaking.

Reality crashed back and he remembered all the reasons this was a *very* bad idea. He didn't do unprotected sex, even while in a trance. He pushed himself up so they sat chest to chest and she looked away. He reached for her and in one smooth motion, she stood. Despite everything, he regretted sliding out of her.

They hadn't used a condom.

She stepped into his sleeping bag, wrapped it around her naked body and lay down.

What the hell? All her stupid ploys of the day came back to him. He'd known she was trouble. Could he have not remembered it?

"Well." He didn't keep the anger out of his voice. "Do you mind telling me what that was about?"

"I think I'll sleep now." Her voice had the slightest tremor. "Thanks."

"Thanks?" he said in disbelief. He stared at her in the

grayness, where nothing was clear except he should never have left his tent.

She didn't respond and while a part of him wanted to shake her, another part wanted to forget it.

Talk about forgetting—Linc. Surely he would have heard if anyone had arrived at the campsite while they were fucking. God knows it hadn't taken long.

He found his boxers and pulled them on, rubbed his face twice, and left.

He didn't care what Veronica wanted. They were going to have a little chat tomorrow before they continued on this trip. Not that it wouldn't have been easier to just not see her again.

Chapter Four

Thanks? Veronica lay awake all night, squirming with embarrassment, if not mortification. Why had she thanked David, as if he was doing her a favor?

Well, that one wasn't too difficult to figure out. It had felt like a favor.

And earlier, revealing her scars, as if he wanted to know. What had that been about?

She groaned and yanked the sleeping bag over her head, wondering why she'd felt compelled to explain how the knife in his palm had startled her. Not that the explanation would have been clear to him. He probably saw it as part of her come-on, or strange behavior. It had been both, she supposed.

Stop.

Turning onto her back, she pulled down the sleeping bag and stared up at the canopy of stars high above. With the coming dawn, their brilliance had begun to fade. The night had been too long but it was ending. Thoughts continued to race through her mind as she tried to understand what she had done and why. She'd liked his touch and kisses. Especially the kisses which had been thorough and deep, as if he had all the time in the world.

And yet, she had rushed ahead, even though he'd been right—she hadn't been ready. Just nervous with thinking too hard and hoping that intercourse would cut off thought. Instead, it had ended the transaction and left her shaken.

She was sorely tempted to escape Veronica, to rise from the sleeping bag and slip into the night, into her wolf's body. David would be glad to see Goldie. But despite the mistakes of yesterday, she could not give up her humanity so easily. Veronica had been gone for too long.

She touched her face, tracing the bones that formed jaw, cheek, brow. Being human felt like a homecoming of sorts and she couldn't let it go. She clung to the sleeping bag she needed for warmth, and she stayed.

Dawn arrived and she was starving. The food had been hauled up into the trees by David and she retrieved it, easing it down on its makeshift pulley, then lugging it back to camp. She sat and munched on trail mix, watching the mist rise like smoke from the morning lake. The familiar sight settled her. As wolf, she'd seen this kind of beauty many mornings. Alone. Not even wrapped in David's sleeping bag. Real wolves would have nothing to do with her and now she knew humans could be just as wary. Both species recognized, at a basic level, that she wasn't of their kind.

Was she unique? That lonely thought made her shiver and burrow more deeply into the sleeping bag. Would David be pleased to know that she took comfort from its leftover man smell? Probably not. He'd been angry.

But not violent. Her fingers came to rest on her three scars. A knife had presumably slashed her. But whose? And why? She feared she would never know.

As the sun rose above the trees, the mist began to clear and the day lightened. Someone within the tent moved. She braced herself for David's presence. The tent door's zipper sounded loud in the quiet morning.

To her surprise Linc, who seemed capable of endless sleep, clambered out of the half-circle opening. His sullen, sleepy face lit up when he saw her.

"Morning," she said, warmed by the pleasure he took in her presence.

"Be back in a sec." He disappeared into the bush.

Veronica swung her gaze back to the blue and white tent. She couldn't hear movement within. Either David was sleeping, or lying still to delay the awkwardness of greeting her this morning. Her heart sank at that notion.

Linc returned, quite cheerful. "Uncle David's still asleep."

"Really?"

"Well, yeah," said Linc, puzzled by the question.

"Hungry?" she asked brightly and indicated the food bag.

He applied himself to making a sandwich, peanut butter slathered on pita bread, then folded in half.

"That looks good," she observed.

He eyed her suspiciously, as if she were making a joke he didn't quite get. Snagging another handful of trail mix, she added, "You guys are generous to feed me so well. It's all delicious." She'd missed human food, though that hadn't been clear until she'd joined them.

Linc gaped. "You like this shit?"

She grinned at his disbelief. "Sure."

He darted her another glance, as if to catch her out. "You're just being polite."

"No."

He took a few moments to process this apparently bizarre information, then shrugged. "I wish we had coffee. I don't know what Uncle David was thinking when he didn't pack any."

"I haven't had coffee for years." She didn't think she liked it.

"Huh," said Linc between mouthfuls and they ate in companionable silence. After a while, he asked, "Do you come to this park often?"

"Well." She tried to avoid an outright lie. "I was here a lot this past year. You?"

"Are you kidding? I didn't want to make this trip. I *had* to come. Because..." His voice trailed off as the tent's zipper sounded in warning.

"Maybe we shouldn't talk about that," Veronica said softly. After David emerged, she nodded vaguely towards him, though she couldn't bring herself to look at him directly until he turned his back to her. She watched his arm move in a semicircle as he zipped up the tent.

"Why not?" demanded Linc. David turned to them and rubbed his face, a face full of sleep. "Uncle David, I can talk to Veronica now, right?"

"I don't think that's a good idea." Despite Veronica's urge to squirm as if guilty, she made herself sit still as David's gaze narrowed in on her.

"What do you know about it?" David's tone was confrontational.

"Nothing." She would not cower. Nor would she explain that Goldie had heard everything. Carefully, she wrapped up the bag of trail mix and hoped neither of them noticed her nervousness, her embarrassment. "You'd rather keep certain things between you and Linc. That's understandable."

"But you're our friend," declared Linc.

To her horror, her eyes stung. *Get a grip.* She placed the bag back with the rest of the food and waited for her eyes to clear. When she could look at the boy without giving herself away, she said, "Thanks, Linc. I'm your friend, too."

Gathering the sleeping bag in her arms, she stood. "Excuse me." She walked off, trying to keep her dignity from unraveling in front of these two men. For God's sakes, she shouldn't be undone by an adolescent declaration of friendship, no matter how long she'd been on her own.

Behind the bushes, she breathed slowly, trying to calm these human emotions. Last night had been her one shot with David and she'd blown it. Somehow that made Linc's offer of friendship all the more difficult to bear.

Once her shakiness receded, she stuffed the sleeping bag in its cover and rolled up the pad David had lent her. So this was a learning process and she'd been wrong about a couple of things. That sex was the best way to connect. That Linc was an obstacle to her reentry into human society.

Linc was her friend. David was her friend, too. He just didn't know it.

ᏚᎧ

David had meant to speak to Veronica that morning and be blunt. Make it clear that, well, he wasn't quite sure now what he wanted to be made clear. *Something.* Like, what the hell happened last night?

But he couldn't just ask the question, especially with Linc around. Besides, the bulk of his anger had vanished when Linc declared Veronica to be their friend and she had fought back tears. He'd watched with suspicion, but her stiff, proud movements had convinced him that she wasn't performing. In fact, she only seemed to perform when flirting.

She wasn't flirting today. Instead, she worked hard as she took down their tent, packed their gear and paddled their canoe as if money launderers were hot on their trail.

Miss Efficiency. David hadn't a clue what to do with this woman with the straight back, long arms and lovely neck. *Stay away*, had been his first piece of advice to himself, but he'd already ignored that.

He kind of wanted to kiss her again. Which was stupid. But right. But *wrong*. Even if her mouth had tasted of nighttime swims. Even if her side was a mystery he wanted to solve. What he needed to do was end his acquaintance with Veronica. Today. They'd reach the access point, drive out of the park and she could phone someone. Or, he'd drop her where she wanted to go.

He hoped she had someone to phone. At times, she seemed too lost and he feared she had no one to depend on. Except him.

"Watch the rock ahead," she warned. They were approaching the shore and David steered left.

"We're almost at the portage." He nudged his dozing nephew with his foot.

Linc, roused from his stupor, sat up in the canoe and blinked at David. The boy could sleep anywhere.

David had slept last night. Despite how things had gone, the sex relaxed him enough to allow for a decent sleep. He didn't know quite what to make of that. It was almost annoying, given how she'd used him. But used him for what? That's what he didn't understand.

Veronica looked as if she hadn't caught a wink. Her face was pale, her eyes smudged. He felt guilty. If she hadn't been in such a rush, he could have made it better for her. They could have shared something. He tried not to stare as she stepped into the water and guided them to shore.

As the canoe slid onto the small, pebbled beach, she pulled it up onto land. Her arm was amazingly wiry for a woman's.

"Hey, what happened to the tip of your finger?" asked Linc, just before she released her grip on the canoe.

She stiffened and gave him a tight smile. "Frostbite."

"Ugh," said Linc, as she curled her hand into a ball.

"Linc." David wondered how marked up the poor woman could be.

"I'm just curious. I didn't say, ugh, because of the finger, but because of the frostbite," Linc explained earnestly. "You barely notice the tip's missing. I didn't until today."

"Sure," said Veronica.

"Did you see when they cut it—"

"Linc!" broke in David. "Enough, for God's sakes."

Veronica dug her hands into her pockets. "That's fine." The jerk of her shoulders suggested just the opposite.

"Get out of the canoe, Linc," ordered David.

The boy watched Veronica who was looking up at their next, steep portage. He gnawed his lip. "I'm sorry."

"Drop it, Linc. And pick up your stuff." David threw everything out of the canoe with something of a vengeance. He hadn't noticed Veronica's fingertip missing and that bothered him. He should know. They'd made love.

No, they'd fucked. And he didn't usually spend the next day canoeing with one-nighters, so he was confused. And more interested than he wanted to be. She caught him staring at her and looked away, then back with some defiance. Hell, he wanted to make love. How stupid was he?

"You paddle well," he told her.

It was relief on her face and he wondered what she had expected him to say.

"Really well," he added for emphasis, then felt a little stupid.

She smiled as if he'd praised her to the skies. "Thank you."

℘

The canoe glided alongside the dock and came to a stop. Veronica jumped out and tied up the canoe. It was not time to leave them, but soon. She felt numb and couldn't quite accept the loss that was to come, the solitude she would have to embrace. Again.

This access point had no phone and David hadn't brought his cell, so he wanted to drive her to civilization. She hadn't been there for a while, not since she could remember—except as an injured wolf. She didn't know how she'd react.

Courage. She ignored the fact that courage guaranteed nothing at all. Because she still needed it.

"I bet you're hungry," David said matter-of-factly.

Veronica stiffened. If David and Linc were any indication, her appetite was abnormally large for a human. She'd probably known that at one point.

"I'm hungry," David added, as if to make her feel better, and tossed Linc a knapsack. "Take that to the picnic table and start without me. I'll get the car."

"Okay." Linc moved off.

"Don't you need help packing up?" Veronica asked David tentatively.

"Nope." He strode off.

Why did she have to think that if only she were more helpful, he would keep her around?

She walked over to Linc and sat. They ate and drank while David packed the car and tied the canoe to the roof. By the time he joined them, Linc was finished eating. Veronica wasn't. It might be her last meal for a while and it was too late to hide her large appetite from them. Soon it wouldn't matter anyway.

"Where are you going?" Linc asked Veronica.

She chewed, recalling the name of the town with Nell's veterinary practice. "Easterton. Can you drop me there?"

"Sure." David watched her. "Do you know someone in Easterton?"

You. "There's a pub downtown, no?" She wasn't a good actor, but she did her best to look as if she were trying to remember its name. "Uh..." She grimaced.

"McMasters?" suggested Linc.

"That's it," she said, relieved.

"Cool. Can we go there for supper, Uncle David?"

"Sure." He still looked at Veronica. His attention would have been gratifying, if he weren't suspicious. "Who do you know at McMasters? I'm a friend of the owner."

Shit. "I don't know anyone. I've never been there. But my friend mentions it all the time."

"Your friend."

"Jen." She was fairly confident Jen was a common name. "I'll phone her and she'll pick me up."

She had the feeling David didn't believe a word of it. Linc began to say something and David stopped him with a sharp shake of the head. The silence that followed was awkward.

"Excuse me." Veronica rose, going off to the outhouse, giving David the opportunity to be explicit with Linc about what not to say to the strange woman who had foisted herself on them. She was not to be trusted. David had, after all, known her for all of a day and a half. Even if Veronica had met him months ago.

David waited until Veronica was out of earshot, though God knows he was tired of having this conversation with Linc. It felt like the tenth iteration. "You cannot tell Veronica you live in Easterton."

By the puzzled look on Linc's face, David deduced his nephew found this directive incomprehensible.

"Why not? She's nice. Unlike you."

She's nice all right. Gawd. David ran a hand through his hair. What did it mean that Veronica just happened to know someone in Linc's hometown?

Nothing. David couldn't believe she had anything to do with Linc's problems, even if she didn't remember the name McMasters, even if everything she said felt off.

"I'm glad she lives near me," continued Linc.

"Her friend lives near you." David leaned forward, index finger pressed against the wooden table for emphasis. "Linc, we need to sort out your stuff. In case you forgot, we have a little problem of bank hacking on our hands. Something the police should know about."

Linc shrank. "They won't believe me."

"Why do you say that? You showed me the text of the threatening email and you showed me what your program found, large funds being moved around. And I believe you." *Pretty much.* David certainly believed Linc's fears needed to be closely examined.

Linc shrugged.

"We need to see what the police make of all this," said David.

"Can't we ask Veronica what she thinks?"

"*No.* N. O. No."

"Why not? Veronica doesn't want to kill me."

"No, but..." But what? David couldn't elaborate.

"You're not cautious. You're paranoid." Linc's face heated up, as it used to when he was younger and about to burst into tears. "She's my friend. I don't have many of those and you won't even let us exchange phone numbers."

"That's right." David sighed, feeling bad for his nephew. "Look, I'll ask for her number. When it's sorted out, if you still want to get in touch with her, you can, okay? Just not now."

"She'll forget about me."

"Then she's not much of a friend."

"You're not much of a friend *to her.*"

Despite Linc's glare, David couldn't bring himself to say, *She's not my friend.* Though she wasn't, just a lover.

"You should let her stay in my house, but you won't," said Linc.

"It's not my place to offer her a bed in your mother's house."

"Mom's away, or she would. *She* likes to help people."

David jammed both hands in his hair. He didn't think he could survive many more conversations with his nephew. "Linc. Don't you understand it is weird to meet someone in the interior without shoes, let alone a canoe?" Though it was more than that. It was last night. It was her desire to work so hard. Her golden eyes.

Under other circumstances, David might have explored the

mystery of Veronica. But now he was responsible for Linc and it was not the time to get distracted by an ill-begotten affair.

"Okay?" he asked Linc, without much hope.

"No, it's not okay. *I* don't care if she's weird. I like weird."

David closed his eyes. *I like weird, too.* "Do you realize we have to get hold of your mother and tell her your story? Can you focus on that instead of Veronica?"

"You just like dumping women. Mom says so."

David froze. "This conversation is over." He got up from the table and watched Linc's face crumple as they walked back to the car.

Well, so much for taking good care of his nephew. As far as David could see, he made Linc feel like shit. And he couldn't even take this directly home to Nell because she and Bob had gone off for a romantic holiday to Quebec City. A vacation she would need to cut short, whether Bob liked it or not.

David packed up the rest of the car. Linc stood sulking while Veronica handed David the last of the bags. Then Linc offered Veronica the front passenger seat. Which was good of Linc, but David wished his nephew's sporadic bursts of thoughtfulness didn't have to strike in such a way as to discomfit David.

They had over an hour's drive to Easterton and he couldn't keep his mind off the dilemma of Veronica while she vibrated in the seat beside him, her leg jigging up and down a mile a minute. Well, she'd been dumped by her boyfriend in the worst possible way, then she'd had unprotected sex with a stranger, and now she had no money or clothes. No wonder she was wound tight.

"Look," he said, despite himself. "If you can't get hold of your friend, I'll give you some money for a hotel tonight. I won't leave you stranded." He glanced at her as he drove, but her expression gave nothing away.

"I'll be fine. Jen always has room for me."

"Do you know that your friend will be home?" piped up Linc from the backseat.

"Yes." Veronica didn't elaborate.

David turned on the radio so he could listen to CBC and forget the woman beside him. Because he was a responsible uncle.

An hour later, they pulled into McMasters's parking lot. As they got out of the car, David made a decision. "Linc, go get us a table. Veronica, can I talk to you for a moment, please?"

Linc stared at David as if he'd suggested he turn cartwheels around the parking lot.

"Linc?" prompted David.

"What do you want to talk to her about?" Linc walked up to Veronica and crossed his arms, as if he had a duty to protect her from David.

"None of your business," snapped David.

"I think it is," said Linc, with some bluster.

David jabbed a finger at the restaurant. "Go!"

Linc teetered on the brink and David couldn't tell if Linc was going to dig in his heels or give way.

"Linc, we'll be in soon." Veronica patted his arm with clear affection.

Which was more than David felt for his nephew at the moment. This was difficult enough without Linc's eyes shooting daggers at him.

"Be nice." Linc pointed his own finger back at David, then turned on his heel and went inside. Thank God.

David walked around the car's hood to stand beside

Veronica. He stared, as if close inspection would give him some kind of understanding, but it only made him feel rude.

He cleared his throat. "I actually intended to be nice before Linc gave me my marching orders."

"I never doubted it." Her sincerity faintly embarrassed him. He wished she would meet his gaze.

"Do you really have a friend from around here?"

"Oh, yes."

"Do you need money?"

She finally looked at him, shocked. "No! I don't want your money."

"Relax. You can pay me back."

She shook her head emphatically. "I just need to phone Jen so she can pick me up after work."

"Let me lend you twenty dollars anyway. I'll feel better if I know you have a bit of cash." It was easier to talk about money than what he really had to say.

"Okay," she agreed slowly, as if acquiescing for his sake. Maybe she was.

He pulled out his wallet and, as he handed her the bill, she seemed to be thinking hard. He waited, curious.

"I just, um." She lifted her hands up, then pressed down, as if to give herself a small boost. "I'm sorry about last night." She winced.

Christ, he didn't want her apology. He found himself catching one of her hands, the one with the missing fingertip. He cradled it between his two and she didn't pull away, despite the slight tremor. Her fingers were strong, yet delicate, much smaller than his own, despite her height.

"Don't be sorry." He smiled, as if that would help. "But you'll let me know if there are consequences, right?"

75

Her gaze clouded with confusion and he had the sickening feeling she hadn't thought about pregnancy. How did one not think about such things? Maybe not in the heat of the moment, but later on. Once again, he felt like Veronica's reactions were off, as if he was missing something that could make better sense of this woman.

"I don't think we have to worry," she said.

"Why not?"

Her free hand crawled to her stomach, but she said nothing. Then her expression cleared. "I don't have periods. I'm too skinny."

"That guarantees nothing." Though it did reassure him a little.

"My doctor says that I'm infertile."

She wasn't looking at him again. Shit. Why was she lying? But he just couldn't interrogate her on this.

"You should eat more," he said gruffly. He still didn't release her hand. He liked it between his two. "Are you"—he searched for the right word—"clean? Healthy?"

"Oh, yeah." She retrieved her hand then and flashed him a big, meaningless smile.

He ignored it. "You should ask me the same question, no?"

"No. You'd tell me if I had something to worry about."

"That's right, I would."

"Okay." She nodded firmly. "Good, that's over. Let's go in."

But he didn't want them to end this way so he busied himself with writing down his name and phone number. "I'm sorry if I embarrassed you." He handed her the slip of paper. "If you're ever in Peterborough, call me."

She didn't look at it, simply put it in the pocket with the twenty dollar bill.

He gazed at her, trying to understand, feeling defeated. "What happened last night?" he asked softly, though he hadn't meant to say more.

She twisted her hand in the air, a gesture that managed to communicate, whether she meant to or not, that something had hurt her. Then she jabbed her elbow towards the pub, to remind him that Linc was waiting for them.

He caught a lock of her unruly hair and rubbed it between his thumb and finger. "You're beautiful."

She looked more lost than ever.

"Would you give me your phone number?" he asked.

She tilted her head, looking as if he'd asked a trick question. "I don't have a number." It sounded like a statement of fact, rather than an evasion. And with that, she walked away.

Okay, that was a brush-off. He thought. Whatever, he couldn't afford to spend more time trying to figure Veronica out.

He was eating, paying the bill and taking Linc to the police station. Afterwards, he would have a long talk with Nell who would decide to cut her vacation short to deal with Linc's problems.

The rest of the evening was going to be a blast.

Chapter Five

Pale, hollow-eyed, smudge-faced, Linc looked about ten years old at the moment. Between saying goodbye to Veronica—Linc had latched onto her as if she were his best friend ever—and visiting the police station for hours and then talking to a frazzled Nell, Linc was exhausted.

Too annoyed to be exhausted, David didn't know if he was more angry with Linc or Nell. Nell, in turn, was furious with David once she learned he'd taken Linc to the police without consulting her. Linc had been threatened so David acted immediately. But that line of reasoning did not placate his sister.

Because Linc had already been to the police weeks ago. A little known fact no one had bothered to share with David. Nor would Linc talk about it now. Instead, he chirped on about Veronica and her fate, jangling David's already frayed nerves. He tried to keep his voice even. Linc was this close to tears and David did not want to deal with a crying jag on top of everything else.

"You saw Veronica come back from the phone booth," David pointed out again. "She even smiled, remember?" Which hadn't reassured David. Veronica's smiles meant she was hiding something, but Linc hadn't picked that up. "She talked to Jen and arranged to meet at seven. I'm sure Veronica is comfortably settled at her friend's now."

"What if this Jen didn't show?"

David's concern exactly, but he kept quiet.

"I wanted to wait," said Linc. "And meet Jen."

"Well, Veronica didn't want us to wait."

"Because of you. You were grumpy."

"I wanted to get to the police station."

Linc rolled his eyes, unimpressed with that piddly excuse.

"Listen, I talked to Tucker. He promised to keep an eye on Veronica and let me know if her ride didn't show. Tucker's dependable."

Linc nodded. Tucker was an old friend of the family.

"It's ten o'clock and he hasn't phoned," David continued. "She's fine." Bit of a jump there, but David was willing to state it.

Linc remained unconvinced. "You took the easy way out."

David surged to his feet, patience lost. "Easy way out? Excuse me, but where the hell have I been for the last four hours? Trying to sort out your shit at the police station. With incomplete information, I might add. Why didn't you tell me you were there last month?"

Linc shrank. "I thought they would listen to you."

"Why?"

"Because you're a computer science prof."

"That doesn't mean I'm an expert on hacking, Linc."

"You believed me. Mom didn't." Linc sounded almost forlorn.

David rubbed the back of his neck. He'd talked his head off, actually, because he had not wanted Linc's story dismissed by the police. "Well, they listened, sort of. But given our busy evening, I didn't have time to invite a woman back here tonight."

"Veronica's not just any woman. Why do you have to talk as if..." Linc's gaze widened. "Do you *like* her?"

"No," said David furiously. "What I'd like is a sister who keeps me informed and a nephew who tells the truth."

Now Linc was standing, too. "*I told the truth.*"

"Then why does the bank insist no one hacked into anything?"

"Because they're *stupid*, like my dad. He doesn't know what's going on. I'll show you."

"Not tonight, Linc." David's anger and energy drained away. What a mess. "You know what the police think, don't you? That you're an unhappy teenager who wants attention. Linc," he pleaded. "I'll give you attention. You don't have to pretend your life is in danger in order to spend time with me."

Linc stared at his feet, deflated. David knew how he felt. "You believed me two nights ago, Uncle David. Mom never did. Or Dad."

"You wanted your dad's attention, didn't you?"

"I didn't make it up!"

David put a hand to his forehead and wondered if he'd ever find the right thing to say to his nephew. Probably not.

The phone rang, breaking in on the argument that had gone round and round in circles. They stared at the noise, transfixed by the interruption. On the third ring, Linc broke the spell and picked up the phone. David hoped it was Nell.

"Hi, Tucker," said Linc.

Hell. Linc listened for a moment before he handed the phone to David.

"What?" asked David without preamble.

"She's still here."

Damn, damn, damn. Veronica was in trouble. He'd wanted her to be okay. "What happened to her ride?"

"I don't know. She hasn't spoken to any woman. She just flirts with the guys, without crossing the line, though she gets them to buy her drinks. Mostly pop." David could imagine Tucker scratching his head. "But..."

"But what?"

"I dunno. This last guy. He's a little more persistent."

"Well, do something about it," David demanded.

"Not like that. It's a bit strange. I think he knows her."

"So? Intervene."

"She doesn't like it when I come over. I make her nervous."

"I'll be there in ten minutes. Keep an eye on her." David hung up.

"Can I come?" asked Linc.

No, was on David's lips. But he saw the scared look on Linc's face again. His fear made David uneasy. Linc wouldn't be genuinely frightened if he'd made everything up. He'd be in his room, role-playing on the internet, not trailing David everywhere.

"Yes." David wanted to keep Linc by his side, anyway.

Linc headed for the door. "Intervene in what?"

"We'll find out." David felt fatalistic. His connection to Veronica was not yet ready to be broken.

✂

Veronica planted elbows on the table and tucked each hand inside the opposite arm. That way Mitch couldn't see her

Jorrie Spencer

shaking hands. She apparently knew him.

"So, what have you done since last year? I missed you." The leer was cheerful, the face plump, the posture friendly, not threatening. He thought she should welcome his attentions. Had he been a friend of hers?

She shrugged an answer, unable to think of what to say to this stranger.

"Do you want another drink? You used to like tequilas."

"No." She'd avoided alcohol all night.

"You like them." He waggled his eyebrows and his smile deepened.

She was torn, wanting to run, wanting to find out more about her past.

"Of course, maybe you haven't forgiven me," he said.

"For what?"

His expression shifted, from friendly to calculating. He took a swig of beer, watching her the entire time. "You had me fooled for a moment. I thought you'd changed."

She frowned.

"But you still don't remember anything, eh?"

She froze. "I remember."

"You don't remember me." Laughing, he reached over and caressed her neck. "Maybe that's a good thing. We can start over."

She stiffened, wondering if this man had carved up her side. Though his hand felt awkward and unwanted, not threatening, despite his change in demeanor.

"You're using that old technique of yours. Saying little, just listening, so strangers can't catch you out, so strangers don't know you can barely remember yesterday, never mind last year."

She was trying hard to think clearly.

"Everyone's a stranger, eh, Veronica?"

She thought of David. "No."

"How's everything here?" The bartender's voice startled her and she twitched off Mitch's hand. A tall, bald, trim man looked down at her with some concern.

"Fine," she assured him. This guy had been watching her all evening and had even questioned her about her ride home at one point. His surveillance made her nervous. She had let others buy her drinks in exchange for listening to their stories. That wasn't so bad, was it? She needed people practice, McMasters had seemed the perfect spot and, until Mitch, the conversations had been pleasant and nothing she couldn't handle. She'd been quite proud of her social prowess.

Mitch ran his palm down her arm and grabbed her hand. "We're reminiscing." He grinned at his inside joke and Veronica found she was irritated more than frightened. Good. She could work with irritation. It was fear that messed her up.

"Yeah?" The bartender directed his antipathy at Mitch, not her.

"We're old friends," said Mitch.

Mitch. She tested the name but came up with nothing. She wished he didn't know about her amnesia. It made her feel vulnerable.

"Are you?" Now the bartender was questioning her.

She smiled vaguely and nodded. She could handle this.

"All right, then." He shrugged and left them alone.

Mitch stole an arm around her waist. "Come home with me, baby, and I won't tell anyone your secret."

The blood drained from her face. Good God, he didn't know

she was a werewolf, did he?

"Hey, I'm just kidding. I didn't talk. Only Steve did. After all, he's the one who got a visit from the FBI."

She looked at him blankly.

"Of course, you don't remember Steve. He didn't want to admit you took off on him."

Now Mitch had both hands on her. One brushed beneath her breast, but she was paralyzed by this apparent window on her past. Steve? The name meant nothing to her. FBI? What would they want with her?

"It'll be like old times," Mitch continued. "Though I'll keep you to myself this time. You can stay for free. Don't be mad I shared you with Steve."

Shared? She jerked around to face him. "Who is Steve?"

"Never mind him." Mitch's roaming hands annoyed her and she slapped them away. He laughed as if she were being cute. "Come on, baby." He leaned over to nuzzle her neck. His breath shocked her awake. No matter what he knew and no matter what she had done in the past, she didn't have to submit to this. She jumped out of his reach.

"Veronica?"

She whirled around to face David. Who was familiar. Who'd done everything a friend would do and more. She'd never been so glad to see someone in her life.

That she could remember.

The relief on Veronica's face almost gutted him.

"Hey." He put out a hand to guide her away from the asshole who'd been groping her and stepped between them. "Is this the jerk who abandoned you?"

"No," said Veronica with a vehemence he didn't

understand.

The guy looked up, a little blearily, from his chair. "Ah, I get it now. You don't need me. You have a new bed and board. Eh, Veronica?" He turned to David. "She pays good." He winked.

David could feel his face burn. "I'm a friend."

"Yeah." The man laughed. "I know about her *friends*. I was one of them." He pushed himself off his chair and stood while the red haze of David's anger concentrated in the fist he clenched.

Tucker materialized beside them both. "There a problem?" he asked in his most laconic voice.

"Nah." The stranger hitched up his belt. He talked past David to Veronica. "You get tired of him, give me a call. I'll treat you well. Mitch Grayson. In the Easterton phone book. Remember, I already know a few of your secrets." He did his stupid wink again and Tucker's hand clamped down on David's shoulder.

"Take it easy," Tucker murmured. "Look after your friend, instead of getting into a brawl."

David turned. Veronica was sheet white, which did nothing to abate David's anger. The jerk was playing with her. But when he looked back, Mitch was frowning as if he didn't understand Veronica's reaction.

"I'm not the guy who carved up your side, baby, so don't put on the terrified act on my account. Save that for your dangerous boyfriends."

"Get him out of here," David told Tucker.

Mitch's hands went up in surrender. "I'm gone. There's such a thing as too much trouble." He turned and left.

"Sorry," said Veronica.

"Do you know him?" asked David, because she seemed so

confused.

She shook her head.

David felt alarmed for her. "How does he know you?"

"I don't know," she whispered.

He gave her arm a squeeze. Someone could have told Mitch about the scars on her ribs.

"What happened to Jen?" piped up Linc, his voice higher and thinner than usual.

Linc. Gawd, he shouldn't be witness to this kind of crap.

Veronica shrugged, at a loss, and David felt uneasy. She wasn't stupid, but there were things she should know.

Well, there were things he should know. Like what the hell was going on and why couldn't he decipher Mitch's remarks? But he didn't have the heart to question her further when she stood as if defeated. At this moment, he just wanted to do the right thing by her.

"Why don't you crash at our place tonight?" he offered.

She nodded without looking at him. Her gaze was diffuse, but it centered on the chair Mitch Grayson had so recently vacated.

&

David finally maneuvered an overexcited Linc into his bedroom. Not yet ready to withdraw for the night the boy's eyes were lit with a crazy I-need-sleep light of admiration.

"You were going to punch him, weren't you, Uncle David?"

"Linc." David rubbed his face wearily.

"Even though he was bigger than you. You didn't care! I saw you make a fist."

"Tucker was there, Linc."

"Yeah, or you would have planted one. Tucker didn't like him either, I could tell."

"Yup. Bedtime, Linc."

"I don't have a bedtime," said Linc, incredulous. "I'm not ten, you know, even if you think so half the time."

Given that Linc was beaming with ridiculous approval, David had a hard time staying annoyed. "It's been a long day and it's *my* bedtime, how about that?"

"Okay," acquiesced Linc, as if he was doing David a huge favor. "I guess I'm tired, too."

David lifted a hand. "Night."

"Uncle David."

"What?"

"Are you going to, you know, date Veronica?"

David stared at Linc. What a stupid question. Well, maybe not so much stupid, as unwanted. "Not in my sister's house."

"Okay." He paused. "You'll be nice, right?"

"Since when am I not nice, Linc?"

"Lots of times. You just don't realize it."

David found himself taken aback by this statement. But Linc stared earnestly, waiting for reassurance. "I'll be nice," David promised.

To his intense relief, Linc shut the door. Phew. Now David just had to get Veronica out of the way and he could sleep. Maybe.

What was going on with that woman? From the clinking of dishes, it sounded like she was cleaning up the kitchen, despite his orders to desist.

Bed and board, Mitch had said. Is that what last night's sex had been about? Hell.

He went downstairs and found her wiping down the counter, which did not make him happy. "Do you want a mop?" he drawled.

She stilled, then laughed without humor. "Whatever."

Be nice, David reminded himself. Linc's orders. "Maybe you should sleep, instead. You look like you need it."

She was worn out, pale with dark circles under her eyes. She probably didn't eat enough, which explained her huge appetite. He realized he was staring and the moment stretched out.

"You slept last night," she said carefully, with a hint of defiance.

"Yeah."

She rinsed out the cloth and hung it over the faucet. As she wiped hands on her jeans, he watched the finger with its missing tip. Then she jammed her fists into her pockets, as if she knew that finger had snagged his attention.

"I like to keep busy, you know? Keeps my mind off other stuff."

"What stuff?" he wanted to know, but she shook her head, dismissing the question. Rubbing his jaw, he waited, hoping she would say more, but the silence just sat between them. "So. I'm doing you a favor, having a dirty kitchen ready for you to clean."

She didn't say anything, just stared. With Goldie's eyes.

What an odd thought. He must be getting punchy. He gave his head a small shake.

"What?" She crossed arms over her breasts. *Very human breasts.* He lifted his gaze to stare at her *human* eyes.

"Why don't you tell me what's going on?" His blunt question

wasn't entirely out of line. "For starters, what happened to your friend Jen?"

"I didn't know her new phone number." The words came out clipped and she avoided his gaze.

He sighed at her lie.

"I didn't want you to feel responsible for me," she blurted.

"Why would I do that?"

Unexpectedly, she smiled, as if he'd amused her. "Come on. You look after people. Your nephew, the wolf, me."

The idea wouldn't leave him alone—she was connected to Goldie. "What do you know about the wolf?"

Her smile collapsed. She hunched her shoulders and stepped towards the back door. Stopped. Her movements were jerky, frightened. Yet he couldn't stop thinking of the wolf and Veronica.

She pasted on one of her big smiles, as if that would shake off the fear. "You're right. I'm tired. Where do you want me to sleep?" There was a challenge in her look and he forgot Goldie for a moment. Was she offering to sleep in his bed? Would she, if he demanded it? *Hell.*

"Who's Mitch?" he asked.

"Some guy. Do we have to talk about this now?"

"You're not exactly forthcoming, Veronica."

"What is this? I answer your questions or I don't get a bed?"

David frowned. "You get a bed, whatever happens, okay? I don't trade beds for favors of any kind. I am *not* your bed and board."

She nodded, then ran a hand through her tangled hair. The T-shirt lifted on one side, showing a sliver of midriff. David remembered running his hand down that side, remembered the

89

smooth and the not-so-smooth skin. *I'm not the guy who carved up your ribs, baby.*

Goldie had scars on her ribs.

"Look at me," he ordered and her golden eyes met his. Angry now. But still golden.

Nell had taken off part of Goldie's toe. Veronica's fingertip was missing.

"Who are you?"

"What?" She was puzzled and frightened by the question. But the idea had grabbed hold and wouldn't let go. He needed to *know.*

"How many scars do you have across your left side, Veronica?"

His heart beat in his throat and whatever he felt was amplified by Veronica's growing fear. Her hands twisted together as comprehension dawned in her eyes.

"Three?" he guessed. "Like Goldie?"

She spun and wrenched open the inside door before he reached her. Only her fumbling with the screen door's latch allowed him to catch her before she slipped outside and disappeared forever.

He slung an arm around her waist, hauled her back against him and slammed the door shut. She elbowed him in the chest. He clasped that arm and turned her round. Her teeth chattered, but he barely registered that as he pulled up the T-shirt to see three scores along her ribs, just like Goldie's, two short and one long.

She went limp in his grasp, while he stared, mesmerized. He really needed more sleep yet he couldn't avoid the impossible conclusion that Veronica and Goldie were one and the same.

"What the hell are you?" He released her. She'd stopped struggling. When she finally met his gaze, she looked devastated. And white.

"Veronica?" He wished he'd handled this with a little more grace. But the shock of it... Before he could soften the moment, she listed to the right. He reached out and caught her.

Sinking to the floor, he cradled her for a moment, stunned, appalled and worried for her. Then he rose, one arm under her knees, the other around her shoulders. Turning to take her to the couch, he found Linc standing in the doorway to the kitchen, face murderous and accusing.

"What have you done to her?" Linc demanded.

"I don't know." His baffled tone confused Linc.

℘

A young, querulous voice rose and fell in the background, alarming Veronica with its uncertainty and fear. Yet she smelled safety. A hand with the smell of David stroked her face and she relaxed. A cool cloth was placed on her forehead.

"What did you do to her?" The voice. No one answered.

She rose out of the mists then, remembering David had guessed.

"Take it easy." His voice was calm and friendly. She opened her eyes and he crouched down beside her.

"Is she okay?" asked Linc.

David and Veronica locked gazes. He *knew*. But his expression was one of concern. She searched his face for anger, disgust or loathing, and found no sign of these emotions. Even his shock had abated.

"Are you okay?" Linc pushed David aside so he had to either rise up and away from her, or fall down.

"I guess so." God, what a long day, and to end with this revelation, when she'd never planned to share her real identity with anyone. Perhaps she'd been naive. She'd left too many clues for David to follow to their obvious conclusion.

She watched David leave the living room and her stomach clenched. What would he do with her secret? A part of her wanted to flee before she knew the answer, but her spirits sank at the thought of running when she'd run for as long as she could remember.

"Did he upset you?" Linc's fierce question warmed Veronica. The boy was a sweetie.

"No. I upset David though." *Really* upset him.

"But you're the one who fainted," Linc pointed out, puzzled.

"That's why she upset me." David returned with a glass. "I don't like people to faint on me. I'm ready to bawl her out now, Linc. I'll just clear my throat first. Do you expect me to hit her, too?"

Linc rolled his eyes. "No."

"Can you sit up?" David asked her in a softer voice. "I brought you some juice."

"I heard a door slam," Linc persisted.

She pushed herself to sitting and David passed her the glass, careful his fingers didn't touch hers. His hand was steady, even if hers wasn't, quite. She drank while Linc and David hovered over her.

She smiled, or tried to. "Thanks. Just what I needed."

"Why'd the door slam? Why'd you faint?"

She decided to answer Linc's second question. "It's been a long day and I was hungry." Hunger had played a part if not the major one. At Linc's doubtful expression, she added, "I didn't sleep well last night. Overtired. It all came crashing down on me."

"Food." David seized on that explanation, too. "How about I get you some cereal?" He returned to the kitchen without waiting for her answer.

"I'm sorry I scared you," Veronica told Linc. "But you can go back to bed now. I'll be fine."

The boy was in his pajamas and had obviously been asleep. "I thought something had happened."

Veronica shook her head and felt an absurd urge to giggle at her denial. As if nothing had happened. She had given herself away.

David returned, cereal box under one arm, bowl, spoon and milk carton in his hands. "Nope, nothing happened." Thank God he was going to deny it, too. Veronica did not want to share her secret with anyone else. "You know, Linc, I wouldn't mind if you stopped accusing me of inflicting great harm on Veronica. I happen to wish her well."

Linc looked sheepish. "It's just you looked angry when I came down."

"I wasn't angry. I was alarmed."

She concentrated on her bowl. No wonder he'd been alarmed. Who wanted to realize their strange acquaintance was a werewolf. Though he looked rather laidback now, for which she felt ridiculously grateful.

"Okay." Linc spoke as if he'd let David get away with it this time. "Should I go back to bed, then?" He stood, waiting for her to approve his departure. She nodded, a faint smile on her lips for Linc, her protector. "Good night."

"Night," she returned.

Linc sloped off with a yawn. Once the boy disappeared up the stairs she found it hard to meet David's gaze. Linc had been a buffer. She couldn't guess what David was going to say to her now, though she knew he was watching. Feeling shy, she applied herself to eating the cereal.

Despite the awkward shyness, relief was her primary emotion. David didn't want to attack her. Or betray her. And while she had no memory on which to hang such fears, she could only assume they were based on something from her past life.

Not that she knew what David would do with her secret. Was this what Mitch Grayson had wanted to trade on? *Please, no.* She didn't want Mitch to be privy to her real self. It would help to be able to sift through memories and to know what people did with such information.

Pass her around? Like Mitch had said? She shivered, wondering if she wanted to confront her past. A clean slate might be preferable.

"Would you like more cereal?" David's voice was careful and difficult to interpret. "You've scraped that bowl clean."

"No, thanks. I'm full. For now." With a weak smile, she handed him the empty bowl and he set it on the coffee table.

"Tell me where I released Goldie last April," he said abruptly.

She looked at him then. His eyes were the color of summer sky. Their warmth, despite the revelation, gave her courage. "McKinley Lake. With Bob, who wanted to radio collar me."

"Well, thank God he didn't," David burst out, appalled by the idea.

She smiled. "I would have been okay. Unlike wolves, I could have removed it."

His gaze intensified and she wrapped her arms around herself.

"Don't look at me like that," he said.

"Like what?"

"Like I'm going to, I don't know, do something terrible to you. I'm not." He sounded fierce, which reassured her.

She found herself tracing her scars through the thin cotton. "Someone did."

"Yeah. I might be more upset if I hadn't met you first as wolf." He gave a crooked smile. "You're not too vicious."

"I don't bite." She knew about some of the werewolf myths, though how she knew was lost behind the blank wall of the past.

"You didn't get"—he waved his arm at her vaguely—"this way after being bitten by another werewolf?"

"I was born this way." Of this, she was certain in her bones. Besides, the dreams implied as much. She'd been a child werewolf.

He watched her, taking it in.

"You saved my life last winter, David. At least I can thank you now."

His eyes widened, as if just realizing she had been in the trap. "That must have hurt."

"The trap hurt."

"Do you not have any friends? Family? Others like you?"

"I'm alone." She looked away because she suddenly felt like weeping. "You've been kind. Too kind."

"I haven't been kind," he ground out with an intensity she didn't understand. "I've been grudging in doing what's right. You deserve better than whatever has happened to you."

She wanted to crawl across the couch and into his lap. But she'd already initiated physical contact and she didn't have the strength of will to face that kind of failure again.

Besides, he was careful not to touch her now, which sent its own message. Just because he took care of her didn't mean he was comfortable with the fact he'd nailed a werewolf.

"What?" he asked gently.

"I'm so tired." It wasn't an answer, but it was true.

He rose. "I'll show you your bedroom."

It only now sank in that he wasn't going to kick her out. "You don't mind?" She winced at the hope in her voice.

"Don't mind what?" That abruptness again. It made her want to stutter.

"That, you don't mind that I sleep in your house—"

"My sister's house."

"—when you know what I am?"

She met his gaze and in it found warmth, not ice.

"No."

Chapter Six

The next morning David was the first to rise, woken by the bright light of morning, or perhaps by the shock that clung to him during the night, even through sleep. He still couldn't wrap his head around the idea that Veronica and Goldie were the same...being. He scrubbed his face hard with cold water, as if that would make things clear. Then he went downstairs to get coffee.

Last night he'd shown Veronica her room and had been made uncomfortable by her excessive gratitude. As if she thought she didn't deserve a bed.

As soon as she'd disappeared behind the door, he'd slotted the idea of werewolf back into the ridiculous pile. It was difficult to take out the shapeshifting concept and look at it with any kind of real belief.

Except she'd known Bob had wanted to collar her at McKinley Lake. And the scars, the missing fingertip, the eyes, all added up to evidence he could not ignore. It also explained why a lone and barefoot Veronica had latched onto their little camping group of two. Part of him was relieved to have an explanation for some of Veronica's more bizarre actions, while another part was poleaxed.

Thinking about Veronica through two cups of coffee didn't make anything clearer. He wasn't sure what, if anything, he should do next.

His reverie was broken by the sound of the front door opening. David jumped up from the kitchen table and jogged down the hall, worried Veronica had decided to sneak away without saying goodbye. Of course she was free to leave. But he wanted her to understand he would help if she needed a friend.

His thoughts scattered as he almost ran into his mother.

"Mom?"

She looked at him, sharp blue eyes under big hair. "Well, you needn't be shocked, David. I do live nearby."

David rubbed the back of his neck, trying to regroup. "Yeah, sure. It's just that it's early."

"It's nine o'clock," she said crisply.

He spread his hands, trying to convey casualness. "How did you know Linc and I were back from our trip?"

"Nell's lights were on last night and I know *she* wouldn't be back. I was driving home from a movie," she explained. "Quite late, I might add, which is why I didn't stop in."

Thank God. Last night had been eventful enough without throwing his mother into the mix.

"It's good to see you, too, David." Despite her irony, she rose on tiptoes to give him a peck on the cheek. Then she reached down to pick up four plastic bags of groceries.

"What's that for?"

"It's your breakfast. Or will be, once I'm done with it." She marched down the hall to the kitchen.

He followed. "That's not necessary."

"Yes, it is. Linc's a growing boy and you don't cook."

"I cook."

She plopped the bags on the table as if she hadn't heard

him. "So, why cut your camping trip short? Did Linc beg to come home?"

"No."

"Then what?"

"Linc should tell you himself."

She extracted food from the bags. "I don't know that Linc's version of events is ever reliable. You know how he is." She looked up and something in David's expression arrested her attention. Her hands stopped moving. "Oh, no. What's going on?"

David sighed. "Nell's coming home today."

Her gaze narrowed. "What did Linc tell you?"

"Mom." He shook his head. He wanted to wait till Nell was here to explain the situation as she saw fit.

His mother planted a fist on her hip. "Don't 'Mom' me. It's that bank stuff Linc was rattling on about a couple of weeks ago, isn't it?"

David crossed his arms, freshly annoyed. "So you knew about the bank, too? No one thought to let me into the loop, even though I was to spend two weeks with Linc."

"We didn't want to bother you about his tall tales."

"Hmmm."

"Linc *lies*, David."

"To his father, yes."

"Well, this is about his father's bank."

"That doesn't mean it's all lies."

She groaned. "You haven't called Nell home because of Linc's stories, have you?"

"Yes."

"David, the girl gets one vacation a year. Did you have to

cut it short? She works too hard."

"Linc's life has been threatened."

His mother slammed two bottles of juice on the table. "You're as bad as Linc, making up grandiose stories."

"When the hell do I make up grandiose stories?" David didn't make up stuff. Period.

"Just because you're not interested in a relationship doesn't mean you should ruin it for everyone else. Bob and Nell were supposed to have a nice getaway."

Now was not the time to say he thought Nell could do better than Bob.

"While the last time you had a girlfriend was in high school," she continued.

Not true or relevant, even if he hadn't brought anyone home, even if none had lasted long.

"If you think I'm impressed by your scowl, David, you're mistaken."

"I'll work on it, okay?"

"The girlfriend or the scowl?"

"What does this have to do with Linc?" David asked wearily.

"You know Nell's a workaholic. Once she's back here all she'll do is work at that clinic of hers. She needed this break."

"I did not phone her on a whim, Mom. I had reason."

He heard footsteps descending and they both looked down the hall, waiting to see who would appear.

His mother raised her eyebrows. "Linc's up early."

Shit. He'd wanted to talk to Veronica this morning, alone, before anyone else was up. Well, it was far too late for that.

"David, you almost look excited," observed his mother. "What's going on?"

"I am not *excited.*" Gawd. He found himself clearing his throat. "We have a guest, Mom."

Veronica came round the corner and paused, unsure of her welcome.

"Good morning." David was embarrassed by how happy he was to see her, especially with his mother looking on with great interest.

"Well, well," his mother said softly.

"Veronica, this is my mother, Eleanor Hardway. Mom, this is Veronica."

His mother walked around the kitchen table with a big smile. "Veronica. What a pretty name. Please call me Eleanor."

The women shook hands.

"Mom's making breakfast," explained David, aware that a hearty tone was creeping into his voice.

"I like to feed my boys." His mother gave Veronica a quick once-over, no doubt taking in the worn-out jeans and T-shirt. "Now, when did you two meet? David never tells me anything."

"Mother. We didn't meet, we just...met. Veronica is a *friend.*"

A small line formed between Veronica's eyebrows as her gaze went from David to his mother and back again.

"David has been kind," said Veronica.

"Oh?" His mother sounded doubtful. David rubbed his forehead.

"He's been very good to me," Veronica added earnestly.

"I see." His mother's tone suggested just the opposite.

Veronica looked confused, uncertain, so she smiled the big, meaningless smile David hated.

"Veronica and I will have a little chat while you finish those pancakes." David opened the back door and gestured towards Veronica. She walked past him and out. It occurred to David she would be hungry so he grabbed a bunch of bananas his mother had bought.

"I'm starving," he informed his mother and her raised eyebrows. "Thanks." He lifted the bananas in something of a salute, then escaped outside.

"Maybe I shouldn't have come down just then. I knew you had company." Veronica sure wished she hadn't, given Eleanor's reaction. Disapproval had wafted off his mother after David had called Veronica a friend, as if the word were code for something else.

David looked irritated. "What, you should have hidden in your room until my mother left? I don't think so."

"Things seemed awkward in the kitchen once I arrived." She had just inhaled four bananas. His mother wouldn't like that either.

"And before you arrived. It's not your fault, Veronica."

When he said her name, his voice caressed her, and she had to smile, even if she thought the awkwardness was indeed her fault.

He smiled back and a small bubble of happiness burst in her chest, warming her. Then his smile faded. "I need to talk to you."

She wanted to beg him to let her stay, which she knew was all wrong. You didn't beg people to like you. They did, or they didn't. She knew that, she really did.

"Do you have family?" he asked.

She blinked at the unexpected question. How to explain that the dream-memory of her boy-brother was all she had left.

Apart from that image, the past was broken and would never be remade. Something had destroyed her memory. Someone had scored her side. And she didn't even know if these two events were related.

"Veronica?"

She met his gaze. "I don't know."

His face gentled. "Did something happen to them?"

She shrugged, swallowing. It was hard to say the necessary words. "I seem to have lost my memory. Can't remember how, though." She supposed it was inappropriate to laugh at her feeble joke.

He leaned forward, eyes concentrated on hers. "Lost your memory? What do you mean?"

"I don't know where I come from. I don't know my past. I can only remember back to last summer."

"Amnesia?" His tone was incredulous and she didn't blame him for his disbelief.

She nodded.

"God." David looked appalled. "Is this common for..." *Werewolves*, but he didn't say it.

"Well, I don't know."

"Guess not."

"I remember the day you found me trapped," she said quickly, in case he decided she was too much of a mess. "I'm moving forward just fine. I can't recover the past, though."

He shifted uncomfortably, as if this was in no way reassuring.

She felt compelled to give further proof of her functioning memory. "I met you and Linc on the portage. You weren't too happy to see me there." She forced a smile, but knew it was weak. *Try harder here!* "See, for a while my memory didn't

103

accumulate. I just lived moment to moment. I'm much better now."

"Hell." He jerked his head to look away from her.

It was okay, she told herself. She could manage without David, even if she'd miss him and Linc. Her next friend would not have to know about all her problems. Nobody wanted to be saddled with this kind of baggage.

"I'm sorry—" she began.

"*Don't apologize.*"

She flinched.

"Please," he added more quietly. "There's no reason to apologize because you're amnesiac. I doubt that was your choice." He reached towards her and stopped. His restraint hurt a little. She was finding it hard to breathe now.

"Why are you trembling, Veronica?" He looked pained.

"It's difficult to talk about this."

"Let's stop for now. It's a lot at once."

She gripped her elbows, trying to still the shaking.

"I just need you to understand one thing." His intensity unnerved her, but she held his gaze. "You didn't have to offer sex to get me to help you. I was already helping you."

"I wanted to," she whispered.

His disbelief was plain on his face. "I don't think you did."

She could feel her face heat up with mortification.

"It's okay," he rushed on. "We don't have to talk about that now either. I wouldn't have brought it up except I need to be crystal clear—you're not trading sex here for bed and board. Not with me. I don't do that."

Mitch Grayson had obviously got to David. Veronica nodded and David's tension lessened.

"I don't want you to feel an inappropriate obligation."

"I don't," she assured him. *I like you*, but he didn't want to hear that.

"You're much too obliging, you know."

"I am?"

"Yes." He looked at the house and laughed softly. "Mom's watching us. No doubt she thinks we're having a lover's quarrel, or something."

We are. But she didn't point that out since the sex had obviously troubled David. Besides, maybe it was closer to, *or something.* "Does she usually like your girlfriends?"

David scratched his cheek stubble. "What girlfriends?"

"You must have had a few."

He cocked his head, studying her. "Now why would you think that?"

For the first time in days, she felt on familiar ground. Maybe at some point she'd been good at teasing. "You kiss well. I assumed you had some practice."

He raised his eyebrows.

She continued. "You have a certain kind of self-confidence that is very attractive."

"Well," he said, flustered.

"You're strong. Muscles are sexy. I'm sure I'm not the only one who thinks so."

David rubbed his chin, as if that would hide his growing flush.

"And—"

"Okay. That's enough."

"Are you sure?" She was tempted to get specific about what she found attractive, starting with his broad shoulders and going down from there.

"You can't really know…"

"If my memory is shot," she finished for him.

He shut his eyes, evidently chagrined. "I'm sorry. That came out wrong."

She knew what he was thinking—she had no one to compare him to, with her memory shot. "Some things I just know." She grinned. "My body remembers, I guess. I bet women approach you."

"Uh…"

"Of course, my body remembers other things, too." At that, she lost the desire to tease. After all, the sex had not exactly been a success. She'd tensed right up.

His expression changed, too. He took her hand and it was such a relief that he'd reached out to her. His palms were warm and large, reassuring.

"My mind doesn't remember," she added needlessly.

"Mitch Grayson recognized you." He squeezed her hand. "He may be able to tell you something."

She nodded.

"I thought it might be useful to ask him a few questions. Maybe he could shed some light on where you come from. What do you think?"

"Okay," she said slowly.

"Does he scare you?"

"No. Not how you mean. I'm scared he knows about me though." Her voice dropped to a whisper. "Please don't tell anyone, David."

He gripped harder. "I won't." His voice was steady, matter-of-fact.

"David!" called his mother.

Veronica jumped and David held on. "Listen, I need to sort some stuff out with Linc."

"I know." At his blank face, she explained, "You told Goldie all about it."

"Right." It took him a moment but he accepted it. "After I'm done with Linc—his mother's coming home today—we can visit Mitch Grayson. If you want."

"Why?" She shouldn't ask, she should just be grateful for his help.

He frowned. "Why what?"

"Why help me?"

"It's the right thing to do." He was puzzled by her question.

David did the right thing. She knew that. She'd wanted him to say he liked her, but it was silly to ask leading questions.

"David!" called his mother again. "The pancakes are getting cold."

"Let's go in." David gestured to the house.

She trailed after him, dreading the sit-down breakfast with his mother who exuded curiosity and disapproval. With some relief she saw Linc was now down to eat. She hoped David's mother would focus on her grandson.

"Coffee?" Linc managed to ask, bleary-eyed, and recently roused from sleep.

"It'll stunt your growth," said his grandmother.

"Don't be ridiculous." David plopped a mug in front of Linc.

"Well, you're not one to talk." His mother crossed her arms.

"My height and my coffee drinking are not related." Amused, David took a sip. "I just take after my mother."

Veronica realized Eleanor wasn't serious. This was their

way of joking, strange as it was. She wasn't used to jokes.

"You're not so short," Linc assured his uncle.

"Thanks, bud."

"Just a little shorter than Veronica." Linc grinned at his observation.

"Yeah. I noticed that."

Eleanor turned to Veronica. "I hope you're not one of those girls who slouch when they feel too tall."

Veronica stared. She didn't know what Eleanor was talking about. "I don't think so." She hadn't thought about her posture much but she straightened her shoulders.

"How's that pancake, Linc?" David's voice sounded a tad loud.

"How did you meet David?" Eleanor asked Veronica in an undertone while Linc mumbled something about the pancake and its goodness.

Trapped as a wolf, didn't seem the right answer. "Just a couple of days ago." Veronica tried to be vague but probably sounded stupid.

Eleanor's expression lost some of its warmth and she transferred her gaze from Veronica to David. "On the camping trip? David, did you meet up with Veronica on *Linc's* camping trip?"

David looked annoyed.

"She needed help," Linc protested.

Eleanor set down the spatula. "I don't know that I approve."

Veronica could feel her face heat up but David seemed at ease.

"Don't worry, Mom."

"Veronica needed help," Linc insisted. "She's our friend."

"Oh, yes." Eleanor nodded knowingly, then shifted her full attention back to Veronica. "And what kind of help did you need?"

Everything.

"Her boyfriend dumped her in the interior," Linc explained eagerly. Veronica hadn't realized how pathetic this scenario would sound when she'd thought it up two days ago. "She asked for help and I made Uncle David take her with us. She didn't have anything, not even shoes."

"I see." Eleanor was clearly puzzled.

His grandmother's two words encouraged Linc to continue. "I was glad we met up because we'd lost our wolf the day before—"

"*Wolf?*" exclaimed Eleanor, while David muttered, "Linc."

Eleanor's sharp gaze was now on David. She waited.

He sighed. "There was a friendly wolf."

"Wolves are wild animals!"

"I am aware of that, Mom. But she wasn't dangerous."

"You can't know that."

"Gran, really, she wasn't." Linc opened his mouth to say more but David quelled him with his gaze.

"Well, there are a lot of tall stories being told around here." Eleanor eyed Linc and the boy squirmed. "If anyone cares to actually give me the simple truth one of these days, I won't mind."

"You're just like Mom," Linc muttered.

David patted Linc on the shoulder. "After breakfast you show me how your program works, okay? I'll see what I can make of it."

Everyone was silent for a minute, to Veronica's relief. She

found the conversation confusing and full of undercurrents she could not follow.

"Well." Eleanor's tone was that of someone trying to mend fences. "Maybe you can tell me why your uncle thinks your life is in danger, Linc."

Linc shrugged and drowned his pancake in maple syrup.

"He got an email threatening his life," explained David.

"Oh," said Eleanor on a rising note, as if she were being told a story.

Linc glared at his grandmother.

"You always did have an overactive imagination. Never mind." She put a pancake on David's plate. "Uncle David will check it out. Maybe someone is playing games with you, ever think of that?"

Eleanor went to give David the next pancake, too, and Veronica realized she was not going to eat more at this breakfast. She tried to keep her mouth from watering.

David glanced at her, then forked the pancake off the platter and onto Veronica's plate. "It's her turn," he mildly reproved his mother who ignored him.

No one talked much after that. Veronica was too busy eating. Linc slunk off as soon as he could. David began to read an old newspaper with keen interest. Eleanor ate one pancake in silence and announced she was leaving.

"Will you come to the car with me, David?" she asked and Veronica watched them exit the kitchen. She ate quickly and decided to clean up.

₭

His mother squinted into the sky before doffing her sunglasses. "It looks to be another beautiful day."

"Yes," agreed David.

"Nell is coming home tonight?"

"Yes. Late, probably. I'll stay with Linc till then."

His mother sighed. "I'm sorry if I embarrassed you earlier."

"You didn't." Unfortunately, that didn't end the conversation, because the apology was his mother's opening.

"I am glad you've met someone. I worry you're lonely. I just don't like that Linc was around. It seems inappropriate. I'm old-fashioned, I know—"

"Mom." David held up a hand. "It wasn't like that." *Not really.* "I put Linc first, okay? Right now Veronica has her own bedroom and it will stay that way."

Eleanor appeared mollified by that news. "I guess you think I'm a fuddy-duddy."

David didn't, since fuddy-duddy wasn't in his vocabulary.

"I don't approve of Bob sleeping over here either."

"For God's sakes, Mom, Nell's been seeing Bob for three years."

"Exactly." Eleanor banged the car once with the flat of her hand. "They should be married by now. Instead, you're calling them home from Quebec."

"Were they eloping?"

"That's not the point."

"God knows what the point is. Look, I need to check out whatever Linc has left on his computer. I promised him that."

"Maybe I should stay and chat with Veronica."

"I don't think that's a good idea," David said hastily.

"Why not?"

"She has things to do."

His mother looked disgruntled. "I should be used to you never telling me anything by now, but I'm not."

"Mom, please." She looked hurt so he added, "Maybe we'll see you tomorrow." Nell would be around then, to handle Mom.

She offered him her cheek to kiss and then, sighing, she got into her car and backed out of the driveway. "Tell Linc I said goodbye," she called.

"I will." David waved until his mother was out of sight.

Chapter Seven

After wiping down the counters, Veronica grabbed a broom. She didn't care if David became annoyed that she did housework. Though it was a reaction she couldn't quite make sense of. Perhaps her desire to work made her appear needy and grasping, a sort of *keep me, keep me, keep me* plea which was entirely inappropriate between humans.

But she liked to be busy. And useful, she admitted. She couldn't sit on her hands while David said goodbye to his mother or talked to Linc about his computer problems.

By the time David returned to the kitchen, she was spraying the kitchen window with cleaner. He stood in the threshold, crossing his arms, and stared at her with disapproval.

Geez, she wasn't committing a crime. Nor was her manner ingratiating. "What?"

His expression eased slightly, to perplexed.

"Why are you cleaning windows?" There was a plaintive note to his voice and she realized that, among other things, he found her behavior inexplicable. She wished she knew how to act human-normal.

"It's something to do." She hoped he didn't see her as too alien. After all, he was an active man who liked to keep busy. That she also believed the more indispensable she was, the safer she'd be, she left unsaid.

"Okay."

She washed her hands free of Windex and dried them. "So, what did you discover from Linc?"

David let out a labored breath. "His program might have been able to find proof of money laundering. If it's as powerful as he believes it to be."

"But?"

David shrugged. "He could be wrong. He could have made it up."

"Why would he do that?"

David spoke like it was an old and painful story. "To get his father's attention. During their last visit, Linc's father was doing an internal audit at the bank. Linc tried to impress him with this new idea of his—a zip program that finds patterns in the database. It's been used to find patterns elsewhere, in music, in writing. He read about it on the internet. Anyway, Aaron—Linc's dad—wasn't impressed. He never is. Puts Linc's nose out of joint. Aaron believes Linc has claimed the program can do something it can't."

"What do you think?"

"Linc did something," David said flatly. "But what, I don't know. If nothing else, I'm pretty sure he stole his dad's password."

"Does Aaron know that?"

"No. Because Linc only admitted it to me when he got scared. The police are checking it out. I don't look forward to hearing from Aaron within the next day or two."

"Oh, dear." She found the whole thing baffling. "But Linc's such a nice kid."

David sighed. "Linc has his flaws, I'm afraid. Stubborn,

among other things."

"What'll happen now?"

"Linc's parents take over. I hope he'll just get a slap on the wrist from the police while his parents lay down a harsher law." He ran a hand through his hair. "I'm still worried about the threatening email. It didn't sound like a joke to me, although that doesn't mean it's not a joke."

"I don't blame you for worrying." They nodded at each other and Veronica wished she could say something helpful or insightful.

"So, what about you? What are your plans?"

She stood straighter, as if better posture would help her. "I want to talk to Mitch again."

"I'll take you."

"You don't have to." She'd rather see Mitch alone, in case David learned things about her that she didn't want him to know. Heck, that *she* didn't want to know.

He stared in disbelief. "I want to."

"Linc shouldn't come along, David, and you shouldn't leave him alone under these circumstances." She was wringing her hands and stopped. "I don't know what this guy will say. I certainly don't want Linc to hear any of it."

"We'll leave Linc in the car while we go in to chat with Mitch." He said the name with distaste.

"No."

"Veronica, how will you get there if I don't drive you?"

She reached for the phone book and searched for Grayson, Mitchell. And found it. "I'm pretty sure he'll pick me up."

"No!"

She was taken aback by his vehemence. "You've done more

than enough. You don't have to be my chauffeur, too."

David banged a fist against the doorframe. "Have some sense. That guy wants to jump your bones and he may not wait to ask for permission."

"I can look after myself." She dared him to say, *I don't think so*, while another part of her wanted to agree with everything he said. That *keep me, keep me, keep me* part. But humans didn't keep each other, for God's sakes. Nor did they appreciate wolf-like behavior in their friends.

Linc appeared in the hall. "Why are you yelling at Veronica?"

"*I am not yelling!*"

Linc glared. "You're yelling now."

"Maybe."

"Maybe? You're just in denial," declared Linc.

David's anger evaporated at that. He laughed, while putting his hands up in surrender. "Okay, no more denial. Sorry for the yelling." He nodded to include them both. "It's just that Veronica has a *terrible* idea."

"I'm stronger than I look," she said. "And fast."

"That hasn't always protected you, has it?" David ran a finger down his side, in a quick, hidden gesture Linc couldn't see.

Linc turned to Veronica. "Don't let my uncle bully you. Even if he usually means well."

"*Usually?* Thanks for your vote of confidence, Linc."

"Is he right this time?" Linc asked Veronica, ignoring David.

"No." She shook her head.

David shifted. "Yes."

"I'll decide." Linc, happy to be at the center of things,

glanced from Veronica to David. His face fell as he saw that neither intended to make him their referee.

"This is private, but thanks for your concern." Veronica rubbed his arm affectionately and he was mollified.

"Don't be mean to her," Linc instructed David.

"I am not mean. In fact, I like Veronica."

"You were mean when we met."

"I wasn't too nice," David admitted. "I had other stuff on my mind. *Possibly* you remember why." He gave Linc a significant look.

"You were nice," said Veronica, puzzled. Both males stared as if she had said something strange. Worse, she saw pity in their gazes.

"People should be nicer than that," Linc told her. "Really."

She didn't know what to say. After all, they'd taken her in and looked after her when she was a complete stranger to them.

"Let me finish this conversation with Veronica." David gestured for the boy to leave. Linc glanced at Veronica who nodded in agreement. With some reluctance, he made his way back upstairs. David pinched the bridge of his nose, waiting until Linc had shut the door to his bedroom. Then his gaze met hers.

"Someone carved you up earlier," he said softly, bluntly. "How do you know it wasn't Mitch Grayson?"

The question made her unsteady. Talking about her scars always did. "A feeling." A weak answer and she defended it. "I trust my feelings. They've been all I've had for so long." While her life hadn't been exactly perfect this past year, she had kept herself alive. With a little help from David.

"I can understand that." He spoke carefully, as if she were a fragile puzzle he had to figure out. "Nevertheless, I can't find

117

that feeling reassuring in this situation."

"That's because it's not yours."

He acknowledged her point. "Look, Veronica, Linc can tag along. We'll leave him in the car where I can see him, but he can't hear us talk, okay?"

"I don't want Linc to know I'm wolf. You knowing is bad enough and Linc might not be able to keep quiet. It's a big secret for a teen. Well, for anyone."

"I don't want Linc to know either. We'll bring along a few toys, his iPod and his computer. He'll be plugged in and totally distracted, trust me." David took a step towards her and his voice dropped. "Humor me."

She couldn't resist his appeal, and she liked the idea of having his support. "Okay."

She thought he was going to reach for her. Instead he stiffened, relaxed and smiled. The smile was compassionate. "What are you most worried about? Do you think this Mitch guy knows you're a wolf?"

It was her biggest fear. "He thinks he knows something."

ℂ

Almost every time David went to touch Veronica, he checked himself. It was a little embarrassing and she no doubt noticed his jerky movements. He had to find a way to stop these odd gestures. This morning's hand-holding had been friendly and comforting, but he was worried about sending her messages that said, *Come to my bed.* Because she would. For all the wrong reasons. Like she would scour the house clean from attic to basement if he gave her the chance.

She was that desperate and he would not take advantage of

her. Too many others had already done so. With time, the situation might change. But right now he refused to encourage another bout of sex that was twisted with fear and this eagerness to please. If they were to ever have sex again, it would bring them closer together, not push them apart. He knew too much about the latter.

Not that he should be thinking about sex while navigating the long, bumpy, pothole-filled lane that led to Mitch Grayson's. Instead, he needed to figure out how to keep her from being made vulnerable by this asshole. Or worry about the damage being done to the shocks of his car. Mitch's house was set far back from the highway.

Five minutes later, they pulled up to a small house which wasn't quite as decrepit as David expected. No paint peeled off the sides, no rusted hulks of old cars sat on the grass. As he switched off the ignition, he turned to Veronica.

"I'll go in," she said.

He shut his eyes briefly. Really, he was not an overbearing Neanderthal who did not think his woman could do anything on her own, but—

"You don't have to come," she added as he opened his eyes.

"I would feel better if I did."

She hesitated for a moment, as if mentally debating the point. "Okay."

Good. He hadn't wanted another argument when she was already tense.

Linc sat in the backseat, obediently listening to his iPod, the racket cranked loud. His long body jostled to the music in a way only Linc could, and David felt a rush of emotion—love, worry, fear. He was seriously concerned about the death threat and no one else was. He'd been paranoid enough to watch traffic behind them this evening, though the road had been essentially empty.

David got out of the car. "Sit tight," he told Linc, who nodded as if he could hear David.

The front door of the house opened. Veronica squared her shoulders while David moved forward, placing himself between Veronica and Mitch who, ready for company, now stood in shorts and an undershirt.

"I don't have enough beer for a party and I see"—Mitch squinted at David's car—"someone else is along for the ride."

"Never mind him," said David.

"The only person I want to mind is Veronica." Mitch leered, rather ridiculously, but it made David grind his teeth.

David stepped up to the porch. He could smell beer on the man's breath. Hardly a sin, but he was glad Veronica hadn't come here on her own. "We wanted to ask you a few questions, if you don't mind."

"We?" asked Mitch.

"Yes. Can we come in for a moment?"

But Mitch only had eyes for Veronica. "Why'd you phone me up and talk as if we were getting back together? Get your boyfriend out of here and we'll talk properly."

David crossed his arms. "I don't think so."

"Don't like your woman to speak up, is that it?"

"Veronica can say what she likes."

"Good." Mitch nodded at Veronica, who regarded him gravely. For a moment, David thought she wouldn't say anything.

"How did I meet you?" she asked, as if their knowing each other was the strangest thing.

Mitch eyed her speculatively. "Kind of like last night. At a bar. You wanted me to buy you drinks. And more. You were hungry and looking for a place to crash."

"Look." David saw that Linc was watching them with interest, even if he still had his headphones on. "Can we step inside for a moment?"

"What for?" Mitch didn't want to budge from his porch.

"I would appreciate it." Veronica smiled at Mitch, full blast. To David's dismay.

"Just you, honey."

She shook her head with a half-smile, no longer frozen by the situation, but in charge and flirting. David could feel his face heat in anger.

"Three's not such a bad number," she added.

"It is with him." But Mitch opened the door.

David wasn't pleased that flirting had allowed them inside. He entered the house first, making sure Mitch backed up so he couldn't grope Veronica on her way in.

"You've wrecked all the fun, bringing this jerk along," complained Mitch.

Before David could open his mouth to question Mitch, Veronica caught his eye and gave the merest shake of her head. Reluctantly, he took the warning and held his tongue.

She focused on Mitch, bright-faced, though David could see the strain. "Last year, did we meet at the same bar as we did last night?"

"No, honey. The one in Shepardsville. And it was the year before last."

At her blank expression, Mitch laughed. "I don't know why you ask me questions when you can't remember a blamed thing."

"She remembers," said David in a low, angry voice.

Mitch stopped smiling and glared at him.

"Mitch." Veronica moved towards him, regaining his full attention. While David steamed, Mitch looked her over, appreciating the view.

"We lived together, didn't we?" She gazed around the messy, dirty kitchen.

"You were here for a good couple of months. I took care of you when you needed it." He grinned. "And you took care of me."

Veronica shot David a warning look before she continued. "So, you knew I had amnesia."

"You didn't just have amnesia, babe, you couldn't remember from one day to the next. You were lucky to have a place to stay."

"I do remember day-to-day now," she said with some dignity. "But I don't remember my time with you. Or Steve."

Mitch looked away, shamed perhaps, though David hadn't thought shame to be an emotion the man was likely to feel. "I shouldn't have passed you off to Steve."

"Passed me off? What does that mean?"

David felt sick and he no longer fought against clenching his fists. Mitch managed to look uncomfortable. "I told Steve not to hurt you. I knew you wouldn't like it." At Veronica's frown, he added, "Steve had a thing for knives. I hear he hurt you."

"Oh." Veronica was shaken. Her confident, flirty persona disappeared.

Despite himself, David maintained an even tone. "Could you give us Steve's name and address?"

"Why? She doesn't want to see him again."

"We're trying to figure out where Veronica came from. What happened to her." *What she may have revealed to you assholes.*

David tried to catch Veronica's eye to reassure her because she hated any discussion of her scars, but she was looking down. Then she turned away and walked quickly outside, letting the screen door shut behind her.

"Hey," Mitch called, as if he still had some chance of romancing Veronica.

Over my dead body. "She's had enough." David sounded calm, though he was furious. "Who's Steve?"

The smarmy look Mitch had been cultivating—presumably he thought it seductive—was gone. "She wouldn't come back here if I'd hurt her, would she? It was clear she didn't like violence."

"Clear in what way?"

"Some guys fought over her once and she got all upset. I calmed her down. She took off on Steve because he hurt her. I didn't. I took care of her. We had a good time."

David didn't keep the disgust off his face. "Right."

"Look, asshole, ask her if she's scared of me. I don't hit and I don't rape, but if a naked woman climbs into my bed every night, willing and able, I don't say no."

"*She had no memory.*"

"What was I supposed to do? She wanted sex. It made her feel better." He actually smirked.

"Then you passed her on to Steve. A class act."

"I was laid off. Money was running low and I couldn't afford to keep her any more."

"Did Steve pay you anything?"

Mitch didn't answer.

David tried not to spit out the bile rising in his throat. "What else did Veronica tell you?" His voice sounded strangled.

Mitch spread his hands. "She had nothing to say. There wasn't much up there. She just cleaned my house and we rubbed along well enough."

Mitch's voice was flat now, weary. He took out a pen and paper and wrote something down. Handed it to David. "Steve MacKinnon's address, if he's still there. He moves around. Don't let Veronica go by herself."

"What do you know about her time with Steve?"

"She went to him in February, a year and a half ago. They were together for less than two weeks. She wouldn't have sex with him, he lost his temper and she took off. Steve claims that, about a year after she left, some FBI agent came round asking about a woman who fit Veronica's description. But, you know, maybe he was making it up." Mitch shrugged. "Steve likes to sound important."

David looked at the piece of paper. Steve lived on the outskirts of town. "He didn't send the agent over to talk to you?"

"He thought it best not to, given our transaction."

David swore.

"Tell me you haven't had sex with her," said Mitch.

David met his eyes but didn't say a thing.

"You self-righteous bastard."

It was ridiculous to have this urge to convince Mitch that it wasn't what he thought. So David didn't.

"You get sick of her, and you will, I know your type, you send her to me. She likes me, even if she doesn't remember."

David left without saying more. The screen door swung shut behind him. He hoped that was the last he saw of Mitch Grayson because the man was bad for his blood pressure. And Steve MacKinnon sounded worse.

Veronica was pacing outside but, as soon as she saw

David, she jumped into the passenger seat.

As David slid behind the wheel, Linc took off the headphones. "Any luck?"

They'd told him Veronica was looking for a friend, which was, in an odd way, not entirely untruthful.

"I don't believe in luck." Veronica rubbed her face. "At least when it comes to me."

In the back-view mirror, Linc's eyes shifted to meet David's, questioning.

"I don't know," said David.

In silence, they drove back to Nell's. David battled murderous thoughts about Mitch and Steve. Veronica, vibrating and anxious, jigged her leg up and down beside him. Excavating Veronica's past had not, so far, been a positive experience.

At home Linc disappeared into his room, back to whatever role he'd been playing before he'd been dragged along in the car. David felt a pang of guilt for not discouraging Linc's addiction, but he needed to talk to Veronica alone.

"What does Linc do in his room?" Veronica glanced up the stairs.

"Flamequest. He plays Aragorn-like characters."

She looked at him blankly.

"Flamequest is a role-playing game. Aragorn is a hero from *Lord of the Rings*."

Her eyes cleared. "That's a book, right?"

"And, lately, three movies." He paused. "You remember general information of a sort. Did you read the book?"

Her smile was small. "I wouldn't know."

David pulled Mitch's paper out of his pocket. "I have Steve's number. Do you want to follow it up?"

"I don't know." She clasped her elbows, rattled. "Not tonight. Mitch was enough, and Steve sounds worse."

"I want to ask you a question."

Her look was wary, but she nodded.

"Were you frightened of Mitch?"

She shook her head.

"What about Steve?"

"The name doesn't mean anything to me."

"According to Mitch, Steve used a knife on you."

"Why?" she whispered.

"Because you wouldn't have sex with him."

Veronica backed up and fell into a chair, unsure of what to make of that information. "Yet I did have sex with Mitch. I can't claim to have great taste."

"Veronica." David wished he knew how to make her feel better. "We don't know that Mitch is a reliable source of information. Mitch—" He broke off because she was shivering, even though it was warm out. "You're cold. I'll make some tea."

"I'm not cold. I hate investigating myself. I *loathe* it. I've had enough."

"Well don't flirt with the next guy, okay? Because I don't think it's good for you and," he added softly, "it *drives me nuts.*"

Her eyes went big. He didn't care what she read into his request as long as she complied. Her big smiles and flirty voice should not be used on subhumans. She was worth more than that.

"I wanted to get information out of Mitch." She seemed buoyed by his concern. "I don't like him."

"Good."

She slumped back into the chair, thinking. As he moved off towards the kitchen, she said, "I guess I was some sort of prostitute." Her voice was filled with dismay.

He turned. "That's a big jump, considering you wouldn't sleep with Steve. I think you were confused." He spoke too loudly, as if that would strengthen the force of his words and make her feel better. And he was almost shaking with rage. "I think you were taken advantage of."

"But I know how to seduce." She looked straight at him.

"So?" He waved off her answer to that. "I'm making tea now. Don't beat yourself up." He stopped halfway down the hall and returned. "Lots of people know how to seduce, you know. Sometimes I do and I'm not a prostitute. You're just very beautiful." That was a bit of a non-sequitur, but he didn't care.

She gave a ghost of a smile. "You said that before."

"Well, it's true. It's also true that what we did earlier was a mistake. But I was certainly *not* acquiring your services."

"How do you know I didn't think you were? Isn't that more the point?"

He stared at her, his heart beating loud. He never declared himself to women. Not even obliquely. But she sat there, lost and alone, looking for something good in herself, and he couldn't hold back. It was worth making a fool of himself.

"In the lake that night, before we kissed, you said you liked me and I believed you. That meant something to me. It made a big difference in what happened because I intended to go back to the tent immediately."

"I did like you."

"I'm glad." He sounded hoarse.

"But I also wanted you to keep me. I thought sex would help bind me to you."

Keep. He disliked the word. "I wasn't going to throw you out like your phantom ex supposedly had. I couldn't abandon you if I tried."

"I didn't know that."

"I told you."

"Telling and doing can be different."

"Not for me."

She was watching him so carefully he wanted to reach out to her. But now was not the time to touch. "You're special, David."

He held up a hand. "Hold that thought." He jogged to the kitchen and filled the kettle, hoping this short break would lessen the intensity before he did something stupid like take her into his arms.

Still, he didn't want her to shut down now that she was talking, so he walked back, trying to radiate calmness.

She was curled up in the chair now, but at least her leg no longer vibrated in panic.

"Veronica."

She looked up, her gaze expectant, not empty like before.

"Don't let Mitch define you, just because he knows something about you, something you don't remember."

Her smile twisted. "At least he doesn't know I'm a werewolf. I'm pretty sure he would have told me if he did."

"Yes. He didn't hold back." David shook his head, thinking of all the garbage Mitch had spewed. "Let's be glad he doesn't know."

The truth was, David couldn't quite get his mind wrapped around this piece of information, golden eyes or no. He found himself looking out the window, then back to Veronica. The moon had been approaching full on the ride home tonight. He

128

felt kind of stupid, but he wanted to ask. "Do you have any relationship with the moon?"

She found the question perfectly normal. "The full moon is my favorite time to run. At night. As wolf. It's rather hard not to run then, actually." She eyed him and he tried to continue as if this were casual conversation.

"You just"—he circled his hand, as if that described anything at all—"change into a wolf?"

"Yeah." Her mouth quirked. "I take my clothes off first." The hint of flirting was defiant and David didn't know quite how to react.

The kettle whistled and the moment was gone. For better or worse. For better, because he could not sleep with this woman until she felt more secure with her place in the world. She'd already made it crystal clear that she would use sex as a bid for security.

She brushed by him and he realized he'd been standing there, clueless, unsure.

"I'll make the tea," she called back to him from the kitchen.

Chapter Eight

"Where are you sleeping tonight?" Veronica stood on the landing.

Halfway down the stairs, bedding in his arms, David stopped and turned. "In the living room." He continued on his way and Veronica followed. He threw the pillow and comforter on the soft couch that was going to make his back ache.

She looked disturbed. "So I've taken your room."

He held up one hand, palm out. "No. I was in Nell's room. You're in the guestroom."

"You should be in the guestroom, not me."

"I don't want it."

She shook her head, as if the world was out of order. "You won't believe the places I've slept this past year. Straw was a luxury. You're used to a bed. I'm not. Being in a house is more than enough for me."

"Well I was thinking of asking you to sleep on the basement's cement floor," he said blandly.

"Huh?"

Okay, bad joke. But it cut him when she asked for so little and he wanted to shake her out of it. She had to take these sleeping arrangements less seriously. He hadn't exactly given her the moon here, just the extra bed.

"Are you suggesting that I can't rough it?" he asked.

"Don't be silly."

"Good. Because you'll just have to get used to living in the lap of luxury, that is the guestroom. I'm not budging from this couch." He flopped onto it. "I've claimed it. It's mine."

She remained perplexed by his behavior, even if she stopped arguing. What would she do if he gave her a gift, like flowers? She'd probably explain she didn't deserve them and try to give them back.

"You're laughing at me." She was bemused, not put out.

"A little." He leaned back, hands behind his head. She was too cute, standing there, and he wanted to give her a hug.

Then the moment passed as she tensed up and looked out the window.

"What?" he asked.

"Someone's here."

The front door flew open and Nell stepped into the house. His sister threw her bags to the floor and kicked the door shut behind her.

"I'm back," she announced unnecessarily and stared at them both.

David stood. "Hi, Nell."

"Hi." After a brief glance at David, she turned to his guest. "Hello. You must be Veronica." It sounded like an accusation.

At Nell's unsmiling gaze, David wondered who had told Nell about Veronica. It appeared the drive home, or the news inspiring Nell's return, had vanquished her good manners, as well as her generally affable nature.

David hadn't mentioned Veronica. He'd been intent on convincing his sister to come home. He'd thought to explain Veronica, or what he could of her, in person. Maybe that had been a strategic mistake.

"Linc is impressed with your outdoorsmanship. He says you handle a canoe like a pro, whatever that means." Nell held out her hand and, after a moment's hesitation, Veronica shook hands.

"Hi, Mom," called Linc from upstairs.

"Hey, Linc."

"Uncle David believes me." Semi-triumphant at this announcement, Linc jogged down.

"Ah." To David's dismay, Nell tilted her chin up. Always a bad sign. "The responsible uncle. Thanks so much, David."

He sighed. "Look, Nell, I honestly think, as I told you on the phone, there might be something serious going on here. I wouldn't call you home otherwise. You know that."

She nodded at Veronica. "We'll see what's going on."

"Nell," warned David. "Don't be a—"

"Careful, you're not allowed to be angry. I earned your undying gratitude, remember?" Nell stalked off.

"What are you talking about?" David called after her.

"I patched up your wolf." Her voice floated back from the kitchen.

Veronica flinched, eyes widening as if she were a deer caught in the headlights. Which was an odd way to think of her, all things considered.

David touched her arm to gain her attention. He spoke calmly and easily, not caring what Nell made of the contact as she returned to the living room with a Coke in her hand. "You're tired, it's late and you don't need to observe our little family drama. Why don't you head to bed?"

"Sure." Veronica jerked her head, gaze skittering away.

It hadn't occurred to David that she would have issues meeting up with Nell again. They had never discussed Veronica's time in Nell's clinic.

Veronica walked around a silent Linc and went upstairs.

Nell pointed to the couch. "Why's bedding down here?"

"I'm sleeping in the living room," said David.

"Not in the spare room with your new girlfriend?"

David raised his eyebrows. "I don't know where you're getting this from."

"I just said I thought they liked each other, Mom." Linc looked confused. "Not that they were sleeping together."

"Great. Swell." The anger in her words was palpable, if misplaced, in David's opinion.

"Nell, I did not call you home because I wanted to take off with Veronica. In fact, I won't leave this house until we find out what is going on with Linc and the goddamned bank. Something, quite frankly, you should have done before now."

"Don't get holier than thou on me."

"Why not? You're acting like a bitch."

"Don't call me a bitch," she said through gritted teeth. "Besides, I'm too tired to fight with you."

"You're calling me worse, Nell."

She stroked her forehead as if she had a headache.

"Did Bob do any of the driving?" asked David.

"Yes."

"All of one hour, no doubt."

"If I want your opinion on Bob, I'll ask for it, okay? At least I've known him three years, unlike outdoor girl there."

David couldn't help but think, *If only you knew.*

"Your non-girlfriend has stolen your pajamas, I see."

133

David had forgotten he'd lent them to her.

"Veronica doesn't have any clothes," Linc put in, eager to explain.

"Ah. That's okay then."

"She's really nice, Mom," insisted Linc, now distressed.

Nell's expression changed to one of disgust. "Or she's taking you both for a ride."

"For God's sakes, Nell, give me some credit, would you?" demanded David.

"Uncle David didn't even want her around at first."

Nell rolled her eyes. "And why would that be, I wonder?"

David wished Linc would stop trying to defend Veronica's character. "You're tired, Nell. Can I get you some tea?"

Nell looked incredulous. "Since when do you get me tea?"

"Now. If you want some," he ground out.

"Yes, I'd better leap at this opportunity." She fell onto the couch. "I take it black." Then she looked at Linc and patted the cushion beside her. "Come here, honey."

Linc sat with Nell and, as David went to the kitchen, he heard Nell say, "David thinks you're frightened, Linc. *That* is why I've come home."

ℴℴ

Veronica tossed and turned, unable to sleep. Nell's arrival changed everything, but that wasn't even the main cause of her restlessness. She was on the cusp.

By tomorrow at this time, she'd be long gone, having shifted to wolf to go running under the moon—and what would David make of that?

On this clear night, moonlight shone down. She sighed and looked out the window. She'd pushed to see Mitch this evening, before her nights were distracted by the fullness of the moon. Its waxing and waning had less impact when she was always wolf. Now her human self had to plan around it.

She threw herself back on the bed, as if that would keep her still. The truth was, she was tempted to leave now, sneak out without a word, avoid any explanation that was due to David. But she couldn't do that to him. Even if the house was too full. Five people were inside now. Nell's boyfriend, Bob, had arrived after everyone else had gone to bed, disturbing David, among others, before disappearing into Nell's bedroom next door. Given her sensitive hearing, they had been impossible to ignore.

By the time everyone fell asleep, she was tense with anxiety. At three a.m., she gave up the fight. She crept out of her room and down the stairs, just so she could smell David and watch him in the gray light of a moonlit summer's night. He lay on his back, bedding kicked to the floor, one arm flung behind his head. His usually severe expression was softened by sleep.

He was so harsh looking at times. Serious. Though he had a sense of humor, despite his impatience. And a hidden tenderness he liked to cloak in gruffness and talk of doing the right thing. She crouched down and breathed him in, relieved to be near him this last night, glad she hadn't taken off quite yet.

She hadn't told him she had to leave. Hadn't found the courage for that conversation yet. Would he wait while she spent her time as wolf?

She feared not. And without David, she'd lose her connection to humanity. Not that another connection couldn't be built but she was growing inordinately fond of this one.

Settling into the chair beside David, the worst of her anxiety eased. In these few hours before dawn, she was safe with him. She wanted to reach out and take his hand, ask for more than his presence. Instead, she let her gaze rest on him, memorizing his features. She may have whored herself out to others, but David was different.

She didn't know when she dropped off to sleep.

ॐ

David squinted into the early morning sunshine, disoriented by the soft cushions he lay on and by the light streaming in through the living-room window. It took him a moment to remember why he was on this awful couch. As he shifted to lie on his side, he saw one long leg stretched out, a foot on the coffee table. He sat up abruptly.

His movement woke Veronica, which he regretted. She didn't get enough sleep. But it was too late, she was blinking owlishly, her golden eyes clearing. They stared, each trying to gain their bearings, as he wasn't fully awake either. He cocked his head in question.

"I must have fallen asleep." She pulled her legs in and wrapped her arms around her knees.

"I know you wanted to give me the spare bed, but this is silly, depriving yourself and sleeping in a chair."

She smiled apologetically. "I couldn't sleep."

"And then you did."

"I like to be near you." Her face stiffened in alarm. "I didn't mean it that way."

His heart turned over in his chest. "What way?"

She shook her head with a small, knowing smile that held

little humor. "You don't want to know."

He stared at her, contradicting her words with the force of his feelings, as if she could read them on his face. "Try me."

"I'm more attached to you than you realize," she warned.

He would have been pleased if she weren't dead serious. "Why should I mind?"

"Because of what I am."

He felt caught in her golden gaze. Entranced. He wanted to kiss her, badly, but he didn't trust her motives. He reached over, palm up, inviting her to take his hand.

She grabbed hold.

"Come here." He gave a small tug, making room for her on the couch.

He was not going to kiss her. Not now, in a house full of people. Not when she was trying to use sex to keep herself safely with him. But he wrapped an arm around her shoulders and pushed hair off her face.

"Is this seduction?" he asked her.

She looked at him, no smile, no flirt, and gave a small shake of her head.

"You don't have to lie about your feelings to get into bed with me, okay? I have certain principles but, given time, I could come to believe you want me for reasons other than refuge."

She looked down at her hands. "You don't think I'm attracted to you?"

Best not to respond directly. "Why this tremor?" He felt it run through her body. "I shouldn't touch you?" Though she leaned into him, not away.

He knuckled her face gently. It was hot to touch. Embarrassment, maybe. "Veronica?"

"I miss it," she whispered.

"You miss what?"

"Contact." She turned, moving into a hug, burying her face in his neck.

"Okay." He didn't know what else to say. *With anyone?* didn't seem to be the right response, but he wondered if Mitch had described Veronica's behavior more accurately than David realized.

He rubbed her back until some of her stiffness receded.

"What if I were an asshole?" he couldn't help but ask.

She pulled back so he could look into her amazing eyes, yellow with brown flecks. "Like Mitch Grayson?" she suggested.

He gripped her tightly so she couldn't move away. Rubbed her back more. Kissed her hair. "I miss contact, too," he admitted, to take the sting out of his question. And because it was true.

"You smell good."

He laughed. "Are you attached to me because I smell good?"

"It's important." She smiled. "But no, it's more than that. You've rescued me three times, you know."

"Three?"

"The trap, the canoe trip—"

"—you didn't need rescuing then. You wanted to..." He faltered. He wasn't quite sure what Veronica had wanted when she'd greeted them barefoot.

"I wanted to meet you before you left the park."

"So, not exactly a rescue."

She didn't answer right away. "It felt like one. I was lonely."

Now he was back to feeling like he was one of many who would do. Because she needed human company and he smelled good. He tried to appreciate her honesty.

"And at the pub, McMasters," she added.

He remembered her look of relief when he'd returned for her there. Her focus had been entirely on him.

"I was so happy to see you." She was talking to his chest now, resting against him. Maybe it wasn't so bad to be wanted for contact.

Her gaze darted down at his tented boxers and back up to his face. He'd been trying to ignore his erection but his gentlemanly ideas of restraint would have been kicked out the window if they'd been alone in the house.

"I want you, too," she said simply. Their gaze intensified. He had to close his eyes to turn it off. "David?"

"Not here and now, Veronica." He jerked his head up to indicate the others who were sleeping in the house.

"I know." She planted a light kiss on his lips and pulled free, retreating to her chair. He let her go reluctantly. "I need to leave."

"You do not need to leave. Absolutely not." He'd never felt so strongly about something in his life. "You stay with me until we get you on your feet, okay?"

"I can't stay. I need to be wolf for a few days."

"Wolf?" he asked, rocked back by this news. He didn't want her gone. She might not return. "Are you sure?"

"Well, yes."

"Oh." He'd assumed she could remain human for as long as she liked. A big assumption, but he didn't know how to think about her wolf nature. "Okay." Not that he could say no, under the circumstances. It wasn't exactly up to him.

"I'd like to come back. Will you be here in a week?" Her hands clasped and unclasped. She was nervous.

"Yes, come back." Normally, he'd try not to sound eager, but her relief moved him. She appeared to think he would cast her out for good. "I'll be here. If something weird happens and I have to leave, I'll give Linc or Nell a message. Though I really doubt that will happen." He didn't quite believe the conversation. "Will I see you as Goldie?" Maybe that would help him process the whole werewolf idea.

"Do you want to?"

"Yes. I'll want to know you're okay."

"I'll try to visit."

"Good." He took it as a definite promise. "Also." He sighed, reluctant to broach the subject.

She observed it and tensed up. "What?"

"Should I find out more about Steve this week?"

She winced.

"I don't have to, but it might be a good idea." He wanted to save her the pain of actually meeting this asshole herself. Mitch had made him sound dangerous.

She drew in a long, shaky breath. "Mitch was bad enough."

He kept his gaze level. "I'll go and find out what I can. See if he has any useful information when it comes to your past."

As she nodded, they heard someone moving upstairs. Their tête-à-tête would end soon.

"When are you leaving?" he asked quickly.

"This evening." She hesitated. "David?"

"Yes?" He braced himself, though for what, he didn't know. More bad news, he supposed.

"Can I wash my clothes?"

He had to laugh, quietly.

"What?"

The Strength of the Wolf

"Sorry. All this talk and then the mundane, washing clothes."

"I live in the mundane world, too."

"I know. I do know that. Sorry."

"Don't be. You've been *great*."

Great seemed like an overstatement.

"I hope things work out with Linc," she said. "He's a sweet kid."

"Thanks." He paused. "I'll worry if I don't hear from you."

"You'll hear from me."

He didn't voice his secret fear, that she was pregnant. He didn't even know if it was possible, given she was a werewolf and he wasn't. But he wanted to keep an eye on her. Despite her experience and perhaps because of her amnesia, she was naive.

℘

Coffee mug in hand, Nell stomped into the living room and took in the state of the couch. "Did you need to have sex in my living room?"

"No. I didn't." David wondered if it was possible to feel more irritated. What was with his sister? That he spoke calmly was an accomplishment. "I told you, she's not my girlfriend."

"Well, your not-girlfriend looks lovestruck to me."

David felt his face heat up. "We just met, Nell. And she's leaving today."

Nell shook her head. "God knows what you're doing. Where is she now?"

"Hanging out the wash. Why are you in such a pissy mood?

Mom thinks I wanted to sabotage your romantic getaway, but I expect better of you than that."

Nell crossed her arms. "Don't be an ass. Like it or not—because I know how self-righteous you can get—it is a bizarre story to pick up this woman on your canoe trip, *sans* clothing, and bring her home after a trip cut short."

"The shortened trip had nothing to do with Veronica. Linc happened to think his life had been threatened. After hacking into a bank. This concerned me. Why didn't you tell me about his troubles earlier?"

She looked out the front window. Her voice trembled. "Just one more example of how I've failed as a mother."

"For God's sakes, Nell, this is not the time to feel sorry for yourself. You need to find out what is going on."

She picked up her coffee mug and drained it. Not that she needed that third cup. She was already wound tight. "You've told me for two years to unhook the internet and I couldn't do it. Now look what's happened."

"Yeah, well he did this at an internet hotspot, not at home, so I'm not sure this self-reproach is relevant."

She slammed down her mug on the coffee table. "The police dismissed Linc's story. What was I supposed to think? That I knew better than they did?"

He spoke carefully now. "What bothers me is that Linc is frightened. He doesn't want to be left alone. He goes for *walks* with me rather than stay at home with his beloved Flamequest. Why would he be frightened if he'd made up a threatening email to himself?"

"To convince you. To get your attention. You barely saw him last winter and he missed you."

David grimaced. It was true. He could have tried harder to

reach his indifferent nephew. Then again, "I dropped by, Nell, and he wouldn't leave his room. Honestly? I don't think Linc would have come on the canoe trip without this threat. He believes it's real. That's my concern."

Nell's eyes grew large. "You're scaring me. Bob thinks Linc just wants attention."

"The wrong kind of attention. A very bad kind of attention from bad guys. I don't think Linc wants that at all." David rubbed the back of his neck. He didn't enjoy making his sister worry, but he felt it necessary. "What does Aaron think about all this anyway?"

She looked at him blankly.

"You know, Linc's father."

Nell's gaze flickered away to rest on her empty mug. "Aaron doesn't know about the latest dustup. Linc asked me not to tell him."

"Why?"

"Because he stole Aaron's password."

"Great, just great. Give me the phone."

"I promised my son, David."

"I didn't."

℘

That evening, Veronica watched the full moon rise early, a white disk in the indigo sky. Despite the moon's thrall, she wanted to wait and shift after the sun went down. It was an effort to hold onto herself like this. But control was important and she needed to relearn it after months, if not years, of being primarily wolf—when shifting choices had been instinctive and rarely thought out.

If she was going to be part of the human world, she needed to plan on a time and place to change. Which wasn't a problem in this small town with its easy access to wilderness. She had little trouble finding shelter from humanity and the right location. She even stored her freshly washed clothes in a tree's hollow.

By sunset, she was shaking with anticipation. She recognized the feeling though she couldn't remember this restraint. The pressure in her body came from deep within and rose until her body became fluid. Her eagerness to be wolf offset the pain.

She embraced the change of bone and muscle and skin. It had only been five days since she'd last been wolf. Under the full moon, it felt right to return to her most familiar form. The world spun as she fell and twisted. Her existence blurred by stretching muscle and organs. Her skin grew thick. Her bones reached for their wolf shape, and she faded out.

Panting, she woke on her side, wolf ribs rising and falling, tongue licking the night air. It was a world vivid with smell and night, a forest silvered with moonlight. Shaking off the last of her human fears, she rose and loped off towards the vast park that had been her home for so long. She picked up her pace and ran, hard and long, under trees, through bushes, over streams. It was a welcoming place, but also an escape. She pushed herself to go farther and for an hour she thought of nothing but movement and the earth upon which she ran, her paws touching and releasing the ground.

Eventually, she had to stop and rest, gulping breaths until she was no longer winded. Her thoughts caught up with her. It had been a while since she'd processed human events as wolf.

Yet she was Veronica more than ever. Because she missed

David, even here and now. The bond was strong, stronger than he'd want to know. At that thought, she raced again, to see if she could outrun her human feelings, but her energy flagged and she could not regain her earlier speed.

There were reasons why she'd hid as wolf. There was a past she longed for and dreaded. There was a man she loved.

Three hours later she was drawn back to Nell's house, wolf in form but full of human thought. It was not as uncomfortable as she'd feared. Before her time as a feral wolf, she had presumably existed like this, torn between two lives, sharing herself with humans and then hiding from them. She wasn't yet ready to let David see her, though she wanted to smell him, perhaps glimpse him through the window.

Nell, ironically, would be happier to see her as Goldie, the injured wolf she'd treated so tenderly. Instead of the random chick she thought her brother was screwing when he should have been paying attention to Linc. David had done both, like it or not.

It was, she admitted, slightly alarming to want to be with David for the rest of her life. The emotion pressed down, overwhelming her. She stopped and sat at the edge of the woods, wishing she could discuss these feelings with someone.

Like the dream-brother who knew what it was to be wolf and human, and to change. They'd been close, long ago. Laughed together and cried. She dreamed of finding him, yet didn't know whether he was alive or dead. Or a figment of her damaged brain's imagination, created to comfort her during her solitude.

David was real. Eventually, to confirm it, he passed by the kitchen window and something within her eased. He hadn't taken off in her absence.

Linc appeared next. She realized the boy was upset, not by

145

his face which she couldn't see clearly, but by his loud, tearful voice. Veronica crept closer to hear better. David had apparently betrayed Linc's trust—something to do with Linc's father—but David, unrepentant, didn't see it that way.

Veronica settled, belly to ground. She watched and listened while people calmed down and withdrew from the kitchen. Gradually the lights in the house went off, until only one remained in the guestroom. David came to that bright window and looked out, arms crossed, body bathed in light. Her heart leapt with joy. As if responding, he took one hand and pressed it against the windowpane, against the night. The gesture was brief but definite. Then he disappeared from sight.

The house went dark. She stayed to watch over them, happy with David's silent greeting, lost in reverie, feeling loyal to the first house that had welcomed her within. Quiet night sounds, frogs and crickets, and a mild breeze comforted her.

Half an hour later, still content and slightly sleepy, Veronica took a moment to register the presence of an intruder—a broken twig and scuffing noises. Her ears went forward and her body trembled. She was no longer the only creature watching the house.

The wind brought his scent to her and the smell of evil had her hair standing on end. Bristling, she rose to her full height and watched as a man crept into Nell's yard and looked at the house. He stayed in shadow, as did she, but while she was aware of him, he knew nothing of her. Her brain screamed danger, not just for herself, but for Linc who was young and vulnerable and under her protection. She threw back her head and opened her throat to bark-howl her warning.

Chapter Nine

The howl entered his dreams and before it tapered off, David was full awake and standing. *Veronica?*

He strode to the window and peered out. The moon was high and bright, but he could see nothing unusual. Then the howl came again, long and insistent. It felt like a warning.

While David pulled on his shorts, she howled a third time. As quietly as possible—he did not want to explain his concerns to Nell—he went down the stairs and out the back door. Then the barking began.

He jogged towards the noise and the barking became frantic. Picking up speed, he tried to get closer but his destination became a moving target. Veronica was on the run. He followed. A branch slapped his face and he managed to duck the next one. He wished he'd grabbed a flashlight but he didn't know where Nell kept hers and his was buried in his car. The moonlight allowed some visibility and saved him from falling on his face. All the while, she led him away from the house, through the woods and towards another subdivision.

Just when he thought he might reach Veronica, the barking cut off. He stopped and found the sudden silence ominous. Then he heard someone run on pavement, a car door slam shut and an engine start, all in quick succession. As he came into the clearing beside the road, a vehicle drove by. After it turned the corner, its lights flashed on to reveal a station wagon, though it was impossible to see its make and color from that brief glimpse.

What the hell was going on?

Standing still, chest heaving from his run, he listened for Veronica. Instead, he heard the thud of his heart and the distant sound of a car. He wiped the cooling sweat from his brow. "Veronica?"

Movement came from his left and he turned to see Goldie walk towards him, her step tentative, her yellow eyes glowing. Relief washed through him.

"What's going on? I thought you were in trouble. Maybe kidnapped by that station wagon."

She stopped two feet away from him and stared, seemingly unhurt. It was the first time he'd seen her as wolf since he knew about her dual nature. The unsettling eyes made more sense, but the rest of her was pure wolf.

"Are you okay?"

She gave a low bark.

"Don't tell me chasing cars at night is your secret vice."

She tossed up her head, dismissing his comment, and walked away.

"Hey! I bloody well need to talk to you. You just led me on a wild goose chase."

She glanced back, hesitating, before she slowly turned and came over to give him one lick on his hand. She bounded out of sight.

David stared at where she had been. Well, at least he could be happy she wasn't hurt. And he could translate that lick into a vague promise if he wanted to think positively. But he wished she hadn't left so quickly.

Tramping back to the house took longer than his excursion out, giving him time to think. With Veronica around, as woman or wolf, it was awkward living in Nell's house. Yet he could not leave Nell's until he was convinced Linc was not in danger.

The time had come to throw up his tent in the backyard. A separate abode, no matter how flimsy, would give him some distance from his nephew and sister, without taking them out of his sights. Then he wouldn't have to sneak out of the house to check on howls and barking. Or explain why he'd chosen to march around the forest in the middle of the night.

Which he was going to do now. The kitchen light was on and Nell stood by the door, waiting for him, waiting for an explanation for his middle of the night walkabout.

"Trouble sleeping?" she asked as he came in.

He went to the tap for a drink of water. "Not exactly. I heard barking."

"So did I, but I didn't go outside and work up a sweat. Of course, I might not have heard the barking if you hadn't woken me by running down the stairs."

"Sorry." He shrugged. "I wanted to check it out."

She gazed at him, unblinking. "Why?"

"Just in case."

She adopted her long-suffering look. "Okay. What did you find?"

"Nothing, really."

"You're a terrible liar, David."

At daybreak, he was putting up his tent. "I heard a car drive away, okay?"

"A car drive away," she repeated, as if he were talking gibberish.

"Yeah." He checked the kitchen clock. "At three-thirty in

149

the morning. I'll mention it to the police."

She glared. "Are you trying to unnerve me with your odd behavior? Surely you've heard cars before tonight."

"I'm worried about Linc." At the dismay on her face, he added, "It was probably nothing."

"I don't know what's going on in your head. But, as I promised you, Aaron and I are taking Linc down to the police station this morning."

"That should be fun." He grimaced at his sister with some sympathy. Mediating between her son and her ex-husband was not really Nell's job, but she got stuck with it.

She ran a hand through her hair, then grabbed a hunk and tugged. "This is what I'll be doing by the end of the day—pulling out my hair. Literally. Aaron is furious with Linc for using his password."

David pulled juice out of the fridge. "And rightly so. What puzzles me is why the bank claims Linc didn't get into their accounts when he did. With Aaron's password."

"You don't know that."

David didn't argue, but lifted the juice box towards her. "Do you want a drink?"

"No. Where's Veronica?" she asked abruptly.

Running around in the woods. "I'm not sure."

Nell adopted her worldly-wise, older sister face. "How much money did you give her, David?"

"Twenty dollars, three days ago. Not exactly a drain on my finances."

Nell frowned. "Don't you think she's a little strange?"

He sighed and crossed his arms. He had thought Veronica exceedingly strange until her secret had come out and he could make sense of her actions.

"She's one of those people who grasp what they can from whoever they can. She's using you, David."

"I like her," he warned.

"Okay." Nell shook her head. "Could you go like her in your own space and not in my house?"

He wished he could. "Right now, I'm going to bed. Alone."

℘

"And you think a third visit to the police station will make a difference." Aaron obviously believed otherwise. Linc resembled tall, gangly Aaron but, in David's opinion, the boy was not nearly as irritating. "It won't. It may cost me my job though."

Nell didn't answer right away. Instead, she passed coffee to Aaron and David, and sat at the kitchen table with them.

"The detective wants to know if something new turns up." Nell spoke quietly, efficiently, as if she were dealing with the recalcitrant owner of her favorite dog. "It has. David discovered Linc stole your password. It makes some of Linc's claims possible, you see."

"This is hardly new," argued Aaron. "Linc did this last year."

"The point is that we didn't know about it last year or even a couple of weeks ago." She cradled her mug in her hands. "You said you wanted to come with us."

"I did. I do," he amended. "But we don't need to bring up the password problem."

"Why not?" Nell bit out the two words.

Aaron didn't answer.

"It's kind of critical, don't you think?" said David. "Since

Linc used it to get into the bank."

Aaron pretended David didn't exist. He just drank his coffee and set the mug down again.

"Aaron, they already know about the password." Nell leaned forward. "That horse is out of the barn."

"Then why are we going in at all?"

"The police want to talk to you."

David didn't know how Nell kept her temper in check.

"If you came here to talk us out of this visit—"

"No." Aaron cut Nell off.

Nell adopted a more conciliatory expression. "Look, Aaron, what Linc did was wrong"—Linc hadn't emerged from his room since his father's arrival—"but the detective, David says, is concerned about the threatening email. So am I."

"David just wants me to lose my job," Aaron muttered into his coffee.

"David just wants to make sure his nephew is okay," said David. "Maybe *you* could think about your son's safety."

Nell waved at David to keep quiet which, considering he'd only spoken twice this morning, seemed a bit much. "David doesn't want you to lose your job, okay, Aaron?"

"I couldn't care less about your job."

Nell twisted to glare at David. "Just *shut up* so you don't make this worse. Please." With false calm, she turned back to Aaron with her good vet voice. "I wouldn't mind some support here. You are his father and, like it or not, your computer allowed Linc access to your password."

"For God's sakes," exclaimed Aaron. "Linc has made this fiasco up. You know how he tells stories that have no basis in the real world."

"Whether he made it up or no, you left Linc at home for an entire day while the rest of your family went out to celebrate your mother-in-law's birthday. I think, though this is a wild guess here, Linc may have felt left out."

"Linc could have come." Aaron refused to take any responsibility. "He didn't want to."

She lifted her hands in exasperation. "You didn't invite him along."

"Of course I did. Do you believe every word that boy utters?"

Nell sighed and David suppressed the urge to say, *Yes.*

"I'm not going to argue with you, Nell," said Aaron. "The point is, he shouldn't have stolen my password."

"He shouldn't have stolen your password," Nell repeated woodenly.

Someone tapped on the back door. David looked over his shoulder to see Veronica standing behind the screen. His spirits lifted, no soared, and he wanted to beam at her like an idiot. He pushed back his chair, rose and walked to her, taking measured steps.

"Who's that?" Aaron's tone implied that Veronica was an unwelcome alien. No doubt her scruffy appearance met with his disapproval.

David opened the door. "Hey, come on in."

She smiled at him, a little shyly, and stepped inside.

"This is David's friend, Veronica." Nell stood to make polite introductions. "Veronica, this is Linc's father, Aaron."

"Hello," she said.

His nod barely acknowledged her and Veronica stiffened. From past experience, David knew Aaron was sneering at Veronica's clothing. Not that David cared how she dressed, but

153

he had to take her shopping. Because people were going to notice that, freshly washed or not, she had exactly one shirt and one pair of worn, ill-fitting jeans. And it was better for Veronica if she didn't draw attention to herself.

While Aaron stared straight ahead, drinking his coffee, Nell walked down the hall and stood at the bottom of the stairs. "Linc," she roared. "Get down here *now*."

"Give me a moment, okay?" David told Veronica in an undertone.

When Nell returned to the kitchen, David asked her, "Do you want me to come along to the police station?"

"No," said Aaron. "That's not necessary."

David tried to read his sister's face but it was expressionless. She looked so tired and the day had barely begun. He wished he hadn't woken her last night. "I don't mind, Nell."

"No!" Aaron stood.

"I'm not talking to you." David kept his gaze on Nell.

"I am going to fetch my son, since he can't be bothered to come down and greet me." Aaron stalked out of the kitchen.

Nell groaned. "Aaron and Linc are enough for me to handle today. But thanks for the offer, David."

"I'll restrain myself," promised David with a tight smile.

She shook her head.

"Okay." He turned to Veronica who stood awkwardly behind him, as if waiting her turn.

"Let me wait outside. But when you have a moment, I'd like to talk to you." Lucky girl, getting to witness his family's shit. He wondered what she made of it, especially when she couldn't remember her own family.

"Sure. I'll be with you soon. Here." David grabbed a bowl,

cereal, milk and a spoon, and shoved them at her. She took them gratefully.

"Thanks." Veronica didn't look at Nell as she stepped outside.

David saw Nell's face. She wore her significant look, which meant she intended to say something he didn't want to hear.

"What would she do if you didn't feed her? Starve?" whispered Nell. "And where did she sleep last night?"

"It doesn't matter."

"You know, I was only irritated by this whole Veronica thing before—extra body and all that. But I've become intrigued by her behavior, and yours as well. Does she ever change her clothes?"

David crossed his arms. "Nell."

"You have to admit it's a bit odd." She poured out the dregs of the coffeepot. "I can only guess that Veronica is one of your charity cases."

"What do you mean? I don't have charity cases."

"Well, I thought you outgrew them when you took on your antisocial persona."

"I am not antisocial. I *teach*. And I do not have a *persona*."

She grinned. "Got you."

He rolled his eyes but he wasn't truly annoyed.

"Remember the good old days when you used to adopt the kids everyone else picked on? Even if you were a foot shorter than the bullies and Mom had to go to school so they didn't beat you up?"

"Nell, please. What are you going on about? Maybe I got into a few scraps."

She sat and rested her chin in the palm of her hand,

smiling. "You pick the oddest things to be modest about."

"You pick the oddest things to romanticize."

"Let me be diverted by the conundrum that is Veronica for a few moments. I need the break." Then they heard Linc and Aaron yelling at each other upstairs, Linc's voice tearful and defiant, Aaron's royally pissed.

"Well, never mind." Nell rubbed her temples. "I'm going to let them blow off some steam before we go out."

"All right." David jabbed a thumb backwards, at the door. "I'll just go chat with Veronica."

He didn't like the way Nell looked at him then, eyes big, mouth pulled down in one corner.

"What?" he asked.

"I'm worried you really like this woman."

"Worry about Linc, not me." With that he left before she could say more. He didn't think he could listen to another Veronica warning without getting angry, and Nell already had two bad-tempered males to deal with.

Veronica settled herself under a tree, at the back of the yard, as far away from the house as possible. That way she wouldn't have to listen to Nell ask about her eating and sleeping habits. Last night she'd been too distracted to hunt. Now she was ravenous. Shifting did that. She was on her third bowl of cereal. Even if Nell couldn't see her vacuum up raisin bran, she knew Veronica had an appetite and that David was feeding it.

If Veronica hadn't felt it necessary to warn him about the strange man in the yard last night, she wouldn't have come.

The back door opened and she looked up to see David striding towards her. He even waved and she lifted a milky spoon to return the greeting, her heart made ridiculously glad by the fact that he was eager to be with her. Maybe it wasn't so bad she'd landed on the doorstep this morning.

She dug back into the cereal, trying to finish before he reached her. It was difficult when her appetite embarrassed her. Yet she needed to eat. As she scooped up the last of the flakes, he crouched down beside her, near but not too near. Unfortunately, she was still hungry.

"Please continue." He lifted the box. She hesitated. "I know about you, remember?" He poured cereal and added milk.

"Thanks." She tried to eat at a normal rate.

"We'll raid the kitchen after the house empties out. They're trooping down to the police station soon."

"I'm eating too much for Nell's peace of mind."

He dismissed her concern with a twist of his hand. "Nell has other worries. Anyway, we'll go grocery shopping and stock up. While we're at it, we can pick up some clothes for you, too."

That stopped her and she looked down at herself. The clothes she wore were clean and typical of what women wore, at least while camping. She supposed she wasn't camping now.

"You need a little more selection, Veronica, than this one outfit," he explained gently.

"I don't want you to buy me clothes."

"I don't mind."

"No." She had no way to repay these favors. Food she couldn't do without, but clothing could be washed.

"You can pay me back later."

She set aside the empty bowl and looked at him in disbelief. "How? I don't know how to make money."

"I don't care about the money," he said, getting impatient. "This is hardly a significant amount."

"I care."

"You'll draw attention to yourself if you only have one shirt." He paused. "Veronica, look at me."

She refused, ashamed and angry that he wanted to buy clothes for her. They were caught in this trivial conversation when she'd come here to inform him of last night's voyeur.

"Hey." His voice was low and caressing and he wasn't even trying to seduce her. No, he was talking about a proposed shopping spree. "Just a few things so people won't wonder."

Nell must have said something. Or Linc's father, who'd been wearing a suit. There was that fear again, of people finding out what she was.

"I suppose I must pass," she said with little enthusiasm.

"It's not so much passing, as not isolating yourself, you know?"

She wished she knew.

He leaned towards her, smelling of coffee and soap and clean man sweat. "I don't care what you wear."

"All right," she gave in ungraciously, though she did feel a little mollified by his last statement. She wished only David's opinion mattered.

He cleared his throat, a tad dramatically. "All that said, I *was* thinking you could do with some underwear."

She had to smile when he glanced at her breasts. "I don't like bras." She didn't think.

"Oh." He scratched his jaw.

"But?" she prompted.

His face darkened. "They can draw the wrong kind of attention. Like Mitch's."

"Okay. I thought they were too small to bounce much."

"They bounce exactly the right amount."

"Thank you," she said primly, tempted to stretch. But ever since he'd decided they were friends only, he didn't like her to tease. Actually, he hadn't liked it much before either. A rather dispiriting thought. The silence between them grew awkward and he looked away.

"Just a few articles of clothing," she warned.

He nodded.

"David." She needed to tell him about the intruder. But the back door opened.

"David," called Nell from the kitchen. "We're going now."

David waved. When he looked back at her, Veronica finally spoke. "I thought we should discuss last night. It's important." She wasn't sure how her wardrobe had become a greater priority than lurking strangers. David didn't even know about the man yet.

"Yes." He stood and reached out a hand to pull her up.

She found herself reluctant to put her hand in his.

"What?" he asked.

"You don't have to touch me, you know."

He stared down at her, his eyes dilating. "What?"

"I've noticed you hesitate sometimes. I'm not sure what that's about. I assume touching me bothers you."

"*Bother* is not the word I would have used."

She wanted to push the issue. "What word would you use?"

His hand dropped to his side, looking weary. "Veronica."

"I know it's awkward that I'm, you know, sometimes wolf. Like last night."

He reached down, took her hand off her knee and wrapped his around it. His palm was warm and welcoming. Smile faint, he pulled her up and didn't let go once she was standing. In fact, he took hold of her other hand. "What are you trying to say?"

"You avoid touching me."

"Well, yeah," he said, as if she should clearly understand why.

"Why?"

"To send you the right message."

"What message is that?"

He sighed. "I have a question, okay?"

She nodded.

"Do you think you should have sex with me if I give you food and if I'm attracted to you?"

Despite his earnest blue eyes, she thought of Mitch, wondering what she had done before, what compromises she'd made.

What was she doing now, for that matter? She wasn't sure of anything except she was falling in love with David more and more each day.

"Would you feel obligated?" This evidently bothered him. Well, it bothered her, too, but it was reassuring that David cared.

"Maybe I'm a prostitute." She didn't want to deal with that kind of past, but she needed to look at things clearly.

He shook his head. "Then you'd be delighted that I'm buying you clothes, not trying to convince me that you can get along with one T-shirt and one pair of jeans."

"Mitch talked—"

"I don't give a shit about Mitch and his opinions."

His certainty gave her courage to speak. "I like you."

His breath bailed out. Like that time at the campsite. When he'd wanted to have sex but he didn't like her. "I am glad to hear that. I like you, too." He brought one of her hands to his mouth and kissed it.

"What are we going to do about us?"

"Go shopping," declared David, closing the conversation, for better or worse.

They walked to the car and on the way to the store Veronica finally told David that a man had been in the woods with her last night. "I think he was scoping out the house until I chased him off."

David tensed right up. "Shit, I don't know what that means."

"His smell seemed familiar. It unnerved me. But I didn't recognize him."

His gaze landed on her before it returned to the road. His hand hit the steering wheel in a simple rhythm while he tried to process her news. "So, there are smells you don't like or trust?"

"I like and trust yours." Especially when he desired her, but she didn't share that detail with him. She wasn't sure how much he wanted to know.

He laughed softly. "I appreciate that, but what do you think the man was doing there?"

"I don't know."

"How close did you get to him?" His tone implied she had been in danger.

"He didn't see me. I was careful."

"You made a racket. He sure as hell heard you."

"I made a racket on purpose, David, to scare him off and alert you."

"What if he'd had a gun?"

"He didn't."

David looked at her doubtfully, which was ridiculous.

"Don't you understand what I am?" she said, frustrated. "I know the smell of guns."

He rubbed his forehead. "Don't put yourself in danger, Veronica. Men kill wolves."

"How can I not know that?"

"Given your memory loss, it's hard for me to judge how much you do know."

"I'm not stupid."

"I do not think you're stupid. However, you were once entrapped by a man."

Traps were different than men skulking around houses, but she decided not to continue the argument. "Can you tell the police about this man?"

"I can say something about the car I saw, and my suspicions that he was at Nell's house." He hit the steering wheel again. "That's it. From now on I'm sleeping in the backyard in my tent. That should keep him away."

"What about *your* safety? Men kill men, too."

He just looked at her, as if that wasn't a serious consideration. As if he couldn't be vulnerable. He seemed wired to protect. Well, his will was something to admire.

She smiled at him. "I forgot. You have me. I'll watch your back."

Chapter Ten

The week passed uneventfully. Linc, Nell and Aaron returned from their visit to the police station without much news, though the police sent a cruiser by once in a while. Much to Aaron's discomfort, the bank was asked a few more questions. Or so Veronica understood.

She was glad Aaron had left, going back to the job he hadn't yet lost. Not that he was dangerous, but he was unpleasant and not particularly focused on Linc's well-being. She didn't see his presence as an asset. Aaron believed this episode with Linc would fade away, if people would only stop poking at it.

As did Nell. Or at least she wanted to think that. But David still slept out in his tent, refusing to decamp, even after Nell told him she didn't want him around any longer.

Veronica had picked all this up with wolf ears. She'd stayed away from humans after the shopping trip. The number of people in the stores had unnerved her and she'd had something of a panic attack. Whether that was her general reaction to crowds, or a sensitivity during the full moon, she didn't know.

In any event, given how Nell and Eleanor talked about her eating habits and lack of clothes, better to wait out the week as wolf. If she stayed, they'd be more than curious about her nighttime forays and her exhaustion during the day. Still,

Veronica did keep watch over David and Linc. David's tent was out there, its neon blue a flag to anyone who wanted to do him harm. She ran in the early evening now, before David slept, so she could guard him.

One evening he came traipsing through the woods and called out to her, his voice coaxing her to come say hello, to let him know she was okay. She stayed in the shadows nearby. But he waited, alternating between silence and broken monologue. She crept closer, fascinated by his desire to connect to her wolf self. Besides, she missed him.

"I can see your eyes," he said, affection clear in his voice. She whined hello, though humans often thought this sound less a greeting and more of a pleading for goodwill.

"Come here. I want to see that you're all right."

She moved forward. His scent drifted tantalizingly towards her, with its promise of trust and gentleness and strength.

"There was a time when you greeted me like this."

Before you knew. She stood three feet away. He didn't move. He just talked about Linc and Nell, and how he couldn't leave, no matter how bored he was.

"I miss you."

She didn't think he would have said that if she were human. David was more open when she was wolf.

"Are you coming back?" he asked, at the end, having run out of words. It was an effort, she realized, for him to talk in this one-sided way, just as it was an effort for her to listen without being able to respond.

Two more days. She moved her nose to the palm of his hand, allowing herself to be patted. It was her way of saying, *Yes.*

It made him happy, this contact, as it did her, despite their different forms. She put a paw on his knee and reached up to give him one final kiss before she bounded off.

"Good night, Veronica," he called after her.

∞

Dressed for work, Nell marched into the kitchen and poured herself coffee. By the set of her body, David knew she was ready to argue while he was ill-prepared and barely awake.

"What?" he asked, before she could launch her lecture.

"Nothing," she said, taken aback.

"Good."

David enjoyed two minutes of silence. He used it to sip his coffee and scan the backyard while Nell rummaged in the freezer for bread.

She got back on track. "Do you plan to spend the rest of your summer here with us?"

"Maybe not all summer." David knew Nell didn't mind having him around per se, she just didn't like his reasons for it.

She put bread in the toaster. "Get yourself some breakfast."

"Nell, I know how to feed myself, thanks."

She perched on the counter and brandished her coffee spoon. "Why are you hanging around?"

He waited to see if she wanted a repeat of the real answer, or if this was a prelude to what she had to say.

"David?"

"Remember the barking I heard the other night?"

"When you woke me up? Yes."

"That still bothers me."

She rolled her eyes.

He wished he could explain Veronica had chased off a man lurking in the woods.

"That was last *week*, David."

"Five days ago," he corrected.

She put down her spoon. "Are you trying to scare me?"

"Since when do I try to scare you?"

"Did you see someone?"

"I'm not sure. Maybe," he fudged. "I mentioned it to the police and encouraged them to send a cruiser by. As you know."

Nell looked down. "I want this to be over."

"I know. But I'd like to hang around a while longer. It won't hurt. Besides, Linc is still a little nervous."

"Linc is a little melodramatic. I hope to hell this teaches him something about consequences, though the parenting books have been talking about consequences since he was two and they've never done me—or him—a lick of good. He has got to stop playing these attention-getting games. He's too old for them. When he stole Aaron's password, I doubt he had visits to the police station in mind. Or even getting bawled out repeatedly by his father."

"Linc wanted to impress his father and he did."

Nell shrugged. They'd been over this before. "So, where's Veronica these days?"

"I'm not sure."

"You're not sure about a number of things, David."

True enough. He wasn't used to being vague. He preferred straightforward.

"You're waiting for her, aren't you?"

"Nell."

"I knew there had to be more to it than Linc." She looked relieved and he decided not to make it clear that he'd stay whether he expected Veronica to return or not. "I guess you couldn't be interested in someone who was good for you, for a change."

"Enough," he warned.

But Nell was on a roll. "You dump the nice ones."

"Yeah. I appreciate you discussing that with Linc."

Her gaze shifted guiltily and she flushed.

"Do you want to deny it?" he asked.

"No. I'm sorry."

"Never mind."

"It was inappropriate."

"Okay, Nell. Now drop it."

She did, gratefully. At least it got her off the topic of Veronica. "Well, I'm off to work. What are you doing today?"

"Biking with Linc."

"Linc hates biking."

"He'll come. He doesn't want to be alone."

Nell's smile vanished. "He's really frightened of being left alone?" She didn't want to believe it, despite all the evidence to the contrary.

"Yes."

She set her dishes in the dishwasher. "Just don't encourage his fears."

"Do you see me encouraging him? Stop casting me as a fear-monger."

Overhead, Linc's alarm clock went off.

"We're leaving at nine," David explained. "Nell, I'm not hanging around to make you miserable. I'm worried there's a problem. You know that."

"Yes, but the police aren't concerned. They see it as a family affair. As does Bob."

Useless Bob. "Where is Bob these days?"

She let out a painful sigh. "Working. He hasn't forgiven me for dragging him back here and cutting short our vacation."

David looked at her steadily. "You could do better."

"I've got to go." She walked out of the kitchen. "Bye, Linc," she hollered upstairs, then grabbed her purse and was out the door.

છ૭

The moon began to wane in earnest. Veronica could feel the difference. It had been almost a week of running at night and this morning she finally felt that it—the desire to be wolf and stay wolf—was coming to an end. For this month.

In her human skin, she stretched, dappled by sun that found its way through the leaves. The lake had been cleansing and while she smelt of forest, she thought the fragrance pleasing. Her clothes, she was less sure about. Retrieving them from the hollow of the tree, she shook them out, then pulled them on. They were damp, but she didn't mind. If David cared, he could give her the new clothes they had bought together.

She walked for a good mile or so, thoughtful, not unhappy, though apprehensive about seeing David's family again. Apart from Linc, they regarded her with suspicion and some disdain. *A gold digger,* Eleanor whispered once and David replied, *What gold?*

That made Veronica smile. David had come searching for her the night before last. He'd missed her, as she'd missed him.

The rest, they'd have to figure out, though she wished it wasn't so complicated, with family and lost memories and Linc's problems.

She approached the house, hoping to find David napping in his tent, as he sometimes did in the afternoon. But it was empty. As was the locked house.

Exhausted by the past week's activities, she retreated to the tent herself. In the midday sun, it concentrated heat. She lay down on David's makeshift bed, taking in his scent. It soothed her, as did the cotton bedding. She fell asleep.

She woke sweating and sat upright, alert to noise. Someone was at the house; they'd rung the bell. Veronica waited to hear them leave. Perhaps a car would drive off. But no, the woman was now yelling hello and marching around the house as if she thought someone was hiding from her. Not a stranger then.

"David?" It was his mother calling.

As Eleanor approached the tent, Veronica combed fingers through her tangled hair. Just before Eleanor's face appeared in the screened window, Veronica let her arms drop.

They stared at each other.

"Hello." Veronica tried not to sound groggy with sleep and heat.

Eleanor's gaze swept around the tent. She saw Veronica was alone.

Eleanor straightened up. "Well, come on out."

Veronica reached for the zipper and pulled it around its half-circle before stumbling through the entrance. "I just woke up."

Eleanor looked her up and down with a slight frown. "I didn't know you slept here. Nell gave me the impression you left town."

"I'm not. I did. I came back." Veronica squinted in the bright sunlight. "That is, I dropped by and no one was home so..."

"So you decided to have a nap." Something of Veronica's discomfort must have shown because Eleanor's face softened and she smiled faintly. "I have a key to the house. Would you like a drink?"

"Yes, please." Veronica was parched.

"How did you get here?" Eleanor rummaged through her large purse.

Veronica didn't want to say anything, answer any questions. She stared at the newly found keys in Eleanor's hand. They glinted in the sun.

"Well," said Eleanor impatiently.

"I walked."

"From where?"

She didn't reply, not sure what to say. *The lake*, wouldn't satisfy David's mother.

"I see." Eleanor disapproved, though of what, Veronica wasn't sure.

"David wanted to meet up again." Veronica tried to sound casual, not defensive.

Eleanor turned the key and looked sharply at Veronica. "No doubt he did."

Veronica wondered if she would get that drink after all because Eleanor stood, hand on the door, as if she might shut it on Veronica's face. But the moment passed, Eleanor was true to her word and soon they were drinking large glasses of lemonade on the back porch.

"This is *delicious*."

Eleanor blinked and Veronica guessed she sounded too

fervent. But after a week away from humanity, and with a thirst that had built since morning, the lemonade tasted heavenly.

"Thank you. I'd offer you another glass but I expect the boys back from their bike ride soon and they'll need their share." Perhaps Eleanor expected Veronica to eat and drink them out of house and home and felt it was her job to keep such an appetite in check.

"Of course. I'll have some water." Veronica went inside to the sink, downed one glass then and there, and filled it up again before returning to the porch.

"What do you do?" asked Eleanor abruptly, surprising Veronica.

What a question. Veronica sat down, wishing she were elsewhere. Because she couldn't bring herself to say, *None of your business.* It sounded rude. And there was no other decent answer to the question.

She settled for, "I'm between projects at the moment." Her leg began jigging up and down. Eleanor looked at it pointedly and Veronica stopped. *David, please come home now.*

"Is David your next project, do you think?" Eleanor asked.

Veronica frowned at the insulting tone. "David is my friend."

"I find that surprising. David doesn't go in much for friends, I've found. He can be difficult to get along with. Except for family, of course."

"David is the nicest person I have ever known," declared Veronica with some heat, not seeing how anyone could perceive David as difficult to get along with. Eleanor, yes. Not David.

Eleanor raised her eyebrows. "Well, I'm glad to hear you say that." Her tone was prim and Veronica didn't know what to make of it.

They sat uncomfortably for another five minutes and Veronica wondered how she was going to escape this awkwardness. Linc and David solved her problem by sailing past the house on their bikes. Her joy was unalloyed.

Linc put on his brakes and David almost rammed into him.

"Linc, what the hell are you doing? Trying to kill me?" David stood half-off his bike after making a hard right turn to avoid crashing.

"Veronica!" exclaimed Linc. "You're back."

David whipped his head around.

She rose, smiling at their welcome. "Yeah, I dropped by."

"It's good to see you. Uncle David said you might come back."

"It's good to see you, too," she told Linc. His delight reminded her of an overgrown puppy. "You look a little overheated there." Linc's face was beet red.

"I'm fine. I'll just put my bike away. Hi, Gran."

"Hi, Linc," said Eleanor.

When Linc pushed off, Veronica allowed herself to stare at David. He gazed quietly at her. Sweat plastered his T-shirt to his chest and his man-smell wafted towards her, a type of embrace, though he didn't know it.

"I'm glad you're back. Stay there." He started to follow Linc to the shed.

"She's not going anywhere, David," called Eleanor.

"Oh." David noticed his mother. "Hi, Mom."

"I've made you some lemonade," she told her son with a proprietary tone.

David wiped sweat off his forehead. "Great. Thanks. I'll be back in a minute."

Veronica realized she was still smiling. Eleanor eyed her and she tried to hide her happiness, without much success.

"At least the feeling is mutual," muttered Eleanor.

ॐ

Gamely digging into his second helping of pasta, David found that dinner, with its heavy silences and stuttering conversations, was painful and best finished as quickly as possible. Veronica had tried hard to eat slowly. While he would have liked to dump a third helping on her plate, she had refused, probably daunted by his mother's raised eyebrows. Mom was using her eyebrows a lot these days and David, for one, had had his fill.

He couldn't wait to get Veronica away from everyone else, though his mother was suggesting tea. Even if everyone was sweating in the thick, still heat of early evening. The wind had died.

Having vacuumed up his plate at a rate that almost rivaled Veronica's top speed, Linc had disappeared into his room with a bowl of ice cream. Veronica looked like she wanted to disappear, too, and David didn't blame her. His mother kept making faces at Nell behind Veronica's back. Had the woman completely forgotten the manners she had taught him as a child?

As he opened his mouth to upbraid her, Nell motioned him to be quiet. David sighed, wondering if they should communicate in sign language and silly expressions from now on.

"What?" he demanded of his sister instead.

"Mom and I are going to a movie."

His mother's face lit up. "We are?"

"Yes."

"Are you sure? I thought you were too tired tonight."

"Your meal revitalized me." Nell stood. "David, would you load the dishwasher? I'd like to catch the early show."

"Sure." David was grateful to Nell for getting their mother out of the house. "I'll even wipe down the table, how about that?"

"You're a prince," said Nell wryly, while his mother said, "Veronica can help you."

"Of course." Veronica jumped up.

David caught her hand. "Hold on. Let's have some dessert first."

"You'll leave Nell with an empty fridge, the rate you're going," accused his mother.

"Mom," said Nell. "David has bought most of the groceries this week and the fridge is full, as you know."

"Good. I like people to pay their way." Before his mother could cast Veronica her significant look—in case that dig had gone over Veronica's head—Nell marched her down the hall.

"We've fifteen minutes to make the movie, Mom." Nell stopped at the bottom of the stairs. "Linc," she yelled. "I'm going out."

Linc immediately appeared. "Who's going out?"

"Gran and I. David is staying. And Veronica, I believe."

"Okay." Linc disappeared.

"Maybe Linc wants to come with us," suggested his mother and Nell shook her head.

"We're going to a chick flick, Mom."

"We are?"

"Linc," yelled Nell again. "Say goodbye to Gran and thank her for cooking supper."

While Linc did just that, Nell came back to the kitchen and scowled at David. "You owe me, brother," she said in an undertone.

"I do. Thank you."

She was mollified by those four words.

With relief he watched Nell and his mother walk out the door. He hoped Veronica didn't pick up how suspicious his mother was. Because Veronica would take it to heart. Not that his mother liked Bob any better. The difference was Bob couldn't care less.

"Why do you owe Nell?" Veronica asked quietly.

"Mom and I don't get on all that well. Sometimes Nell chooses to separate us." He didn't add that his mother had been rude to Veronica. She'd decided Veronica was taking him for a ride. Which was ironic. For the last ten years his mother had claimed he didn't treat girls—always girls—well enough to keep any around.

It was all amusing, or would have been if he wasn't so annoyed. Veronica's scruffy clothes, large appetite and apparent lack of personal history—*Is she homeless?* his mother had hissed at him with Veronica still in earshot—all convinced his mother Veronica was using him for bed and board.

He wished his mother wasn't echoing Mitch. It made him uneasy. Because he didn't trust his judgment when it came to women. It had always been that way, except when he looked into Veronica's honest face.

"Your mother isn't too impressed with me," Veronica ventured.

"Don't mind Mom."

"I guess I'm not good enough?" The question seemed to be one of curiosity. "I told her we were friends, you see."

"We are friends, but she thinks it's code for something else."

"Really?"

"Look, let's get you more to eat before we lose our appetites discussing my mother."

"Are you really hungry?"

"I biked all day, so yeah." Though if Veronica stayed around and he continued to match her intake, he'd expand quickly. "I guess you're hungry from being wolf."

Her smile was faint and ironic, as if his question were naive. "The hungriest."

୫

After Nell and Eleanor left, Linc came down for more dessert. The three of them sat around the kitchen talking and eating their fill of ice cream. It was silly to feel more at ease because Linc and David were unusually hungry after their active day. Nevertheless, Veronica liked that their appetites were in line with hers.

Mostly Linc talked while she and David listened to descriptions of his current Flamequest game. David followed the thread of the conversation while Veronica only understood that Linc's favorite character was sword-wielding and clever. They all trooped up to Linc's room at one point to watch some of the game, while Linc gave a running commentary which David punctuated with appropriate questions.

Linc's avatar, Veronica noted, was heavily muscled but not interested in girls. As Linc became engrossed in his role, she and David left the room. He beckoned her over to the guestroom.

"Here you go. And your new clothes are on your bed."

She stared at the single bed. "I thought I'd sleep in your tent."

"No. That's where I sleep."

"I know that." He didn't want her there and she wasn't going to beg to be with him. But. "I'm sure Nell will be pleased I'm staying in her house overnight again."

Veronica thought about leaving Nell's for good. Linc and David were great. Nell and Eleanor, not so much. Maybe later on she could look up David at his place in Peterborough.

"Hey." David rubbed her arm. "I wouldn't put you in here if Nell really minded. Honest. She has a lot on her plate right now so she's grumpy."

Despite her best intentions, Veronica said, "I like being with you."

He smiled, pleased, as if he hadn't been entirely sure of this point before. Which was ridiculous. "Good. Let's sit out on the porch before the bugs get too bad."

They settled on the bench together which, Veronica supposed, was a step up from David sitting on the chair across from her. In low voices, they talked of what they had done during their past week apart. Veronica listened more than talked. She had little to say about her forest life and still wasn't sure how David felt about her double nature. He tended to forget she was werewolf. That idea made her tense up and she couldn't relax again.

"Veronica?"

She jerked her head up. "Sorry. I'm overwhelmed."

"With?"

"Being back. With humans. Not you," she added, given his frown. "But the others. Your mom and sister."

He cast about for something to say. "Are you hungry?" As if feeding her would make things right.

She had to laugh. "Not quite yet. I'm not that voracious."

He was watching her. That's what got her the most. He wanted her. She could smell it. But he also thought his desire misplaced.

He gestured, palm up, to ask what was wrong.

"I won't be able to sleep in that room upstairs."

"Why not?"

Her smile was slight, she knew.

"No," he said.

"Why not?"

"You just want to please me and it's not necessary."

It sure felt necessary. She didn't release his gaze and she could feel his resolve crumbling. Her smile widened.

"You don't need to…" He searched for words.

"It's not like that." She didn't want him to describe sex as something she was trying to barter with.

"It was."

"Not exactly. I wanted to connect. Remember, I knew you from months ago, even if you didn't know me. And things between us have changed a lot since last week. You know what I am."

"I can't have sex with you."

She deflated, fearing she'd misjudged his feelings.

"*No,*" he said with that intensity she loved. "Don't look like that."

"Don't feel sorry for me, then."

He reached for her, his two large hands on her shoulders, their warmth seeping through the thin cotton. "You didn't enjoy it last time, remember?"

"I don't care." She froze because she'd said exactly the wrong thing.

"I care." He was relieved she had given him an out, or a way to explain. She hadn't wanted to give him either. "Because I care about you. It's not right to make love with your memory loss."

She touched his hand, running her fingers over his knuckles, feathering the tendons that ran back to his thick wrist. "When I said I didn't care, I meant I liked you holding and kissing me. I think of that often. It was important to me."

He went still. She felt like she'd found the key she needed to unlock a treasure.

"David?"

"Okay," he said, his voice rough.

"Okay?" She wasn't sure what, exactly, was okay, though it sounded promising.

He gathered her in his arms. "We can do that, the holding and kissing part."

Chapter Eleven

His arms came around her and he pulled her close, wrapping her in his warmth. She let out a sigh of relief. It had been forever since she'd been embraced by someone she trusted. The last time he'd held her, there'd been like on her side, and hope, but not the knowledge she could trust him as Veronica. If she could only lie with him, skin to skin, she would be healed.

That wasn't true. There were more problems to be solved than her need for contact. But she had been alone too long and touch deprivation had done damage.

Edging closer, she laid her head on his shoulder and breathed on his neck. His tension eased when she kissed the tendon that ran up from his shoulder. When she nuzzled him, he held her even more firmly in his grasp, strong arms encircling her, large hand splayed over her ribs. Cotton lay between them and she wished they were naked.

As if reading her mind, David's hand dipped lower, beneath the hem of her shirt, and slid against her skin. She pulled back slightly, smiling. "This feels so good."

"Yeah?"

"You holding me," she elaborated. "I like it. I like you."

His eyes darkened and his breathing became a little more labored. "We can do the holding thing."

A giggle escaped her. "I like the kissing thing, too, David."

"Right." He slid a hand through her hair, it came to rest at the back of her neck, and he brought her mouth slowly to his.

Lips touched, chaste, sweet movements. His tension was, in part, because he focused on being careful. They had never really discussed their first encounter, but he knew she'd become frightened.

She wanted to show him there was no fear now, just the feel of his warm lips and his hours-old stubble that wasn't sharp enough to scratch.

So she caught his lower lip with her teeth and tugged. He sat up and stared at her in the gathering dark, trying to decipher that action, and she smiled. His eyes seemed to change with the sky, turning a deep blue. His hand caught her chin and his mouth came down on hers, opening her up. Her body sang, *Yes.*

She tried not to meet his kisses with desperation, tried to respond in kind, for there was a gathering hum of pleasure in his throat, and she could feel the delight with which he kissed her so thoroughly.

Turning in his arms, she maneuvered to straddle him on the bench, her knees on the wooden slats, her rump on his knees. If she nudged forward she could press against his erection. *Not yet,* something warned her. His hands roamed her skin, stroked her back, traced her spinal column, distracting her with their warm touch and their dancing message of affection.

He broke the kiss and his mouth explored her neck. Shivering with pleasure, she searched for more of his skin. She undid the top of his shirt and found muscle and hair that she had so briefly embraced on that lake days ago.

"Hey," he murmured, grabbing her hands to stop her work

on his buttons. "I don't really want Linc to find me half-dressed here."

She looked down. "I just like skin."

He pressed his forehead against hers and ran hands through her hair and down her neck and shoulders. They breathed each other in.

"Not anyone's skin," she added, because he thought she had no ability to discriminate. "Yours." She trailed fingers up his arm. "I like your arms. They're twice as thick as mine. How did that happen? I do a *lot* of running."

He just smiled.

Her palm swept up, feeling the blond shadow of his stubble. "I like how quickly the hair grows back in. It fascinates me. And"—she placed her hands on his chest—"this part is solid and safe and warm."

He was mildly embarrassed by her praise, which she took note of for the future. He kissed her again, this time holding her hands gently in his. She let herself be captured in this way. His tongue explored hers and a languorous haze descended upon her body, leaving her in a trance.

Then something shifted and urgency mounted. He let go of her hands and his palm rose, seeking her breast, heat against her nipple. He groaned and she pressed against his erection, his shorts damp now. That discovery made her smile into his mouth.

He broke off the kiss and crushed her to him. "We have to stop," he rasped.

She didn't move, thinking hard. She could convince him to continue, she knew it. He was close. But she nodded, choosing to agree. Because of Linc, because she didn't want David's regrets and because later they would have time together without fear of discovery. She slowly disengaged, feeling wobbly and silly and happy.

"I really like you, David." She didn't care if she was repeating herself. "A lot," she added, in case that wasn't sufficient.

But he looked at her so seriously that her happiness collapsed, suddenly invaded by doubts that were never all that far away.

"What?"

He shook his head. "I'm not sure what we're doing here. Was that holding and kissing?"

"Well yes, but..."

"But perhaps a bit more." He was amused now, and she relaxed. He looked at his shorts. "Hell," he swore in resignation and stood, lifting her in the process. He placed her beside him, then tugged on his shirt in an attempt to cover the damp evidence of their recent activity.

She laughed and he eyed her.

"I feel like a fifteen-year-old," he said, "expecting the girl's parents to come out on the porch any minute. Except now it's my family I'm concerned about and for different reasons."

"You're fine."

He looked doubtful. "This is why I prefer to make out at home, not at my sister's with my mother and nephew hanging around."

"I wonder if I did this at fifteen." They both stopped smiling. "I wish I knew," she explained, sorry to ruin their playful mood.

"So do I." He caught her hand and kissed her palm. They were back to being serious. "I'm not sure what I'm going to do with you."

She shrank a little. She didn't want him thinking of her as a burden.

"Hey," he said to rally her, but she looked off in the distance. She'd have to remember touch didn't solve problems, even if it made her feel good.

The doorbell rang. David straightened, tugging on his shirt again.

"No one will notice," Veronica assured him, as she combed fingers through her hair. Her face and lips felt warm though. It would be evident they'd been kissing once she entered the brightness of the kitchen.

They heard Linc run down the stairs.

"I need to see who is here." David strode into the house while Veronica heard Linc exchange words with someone. A male voice and not Bob's. Veronica took a deep breath and followed David in. Her eyes narrowed against the electric light in the kitchen. After sunset, she preferred dark.

"Uncle David?" Linc sounded nervous.

"I'm right here, bud."

Then Veronica emerged from the hall to see that Linc's arms were crossed. He was hunched over, gnawing his lower lip.

Barely glancing at the man who stood outside on the front step, she walked over to pat Linc's arm in reassurance. The stranger's scent wafted towards her and the last of lust and warmth fled Veronica's body.

"This guy says he wants to see you," Linc told Veronica in a low voice.

She made herself face the man. She'd thought this call was about Linc, but the smell was familiar.

"Yes?" demanded David, his voice curt.

The man, blond, scruffy, but not unattractive, ignored David and smiled at Veronica. "It is you. I didn't believe Mitch."

"Who are you?" David stepped across so he stood between Veronica and the man.

"I'm Steve." He looked past David's shoulder at Veronica. "What a coincidence, to find you with Linc. Or maybe not. After all, you've both had trouble with the law."

"I don't think so," said David.

"I hear you don't remember me," continued Steve. "But I know you well. You had me worried when you disappeared."

She breathed in, to make sure. There was no doubt in her mind. This man had lurked outside the house a week ago. Which didn't make any sense if the lurker was connected to Linc and his computer problems. Since Steve was focused on her. Or was he? Steve winked at a nervous Linc.

"I'll bet you were worried." David sounded furious. "Worried that she'd go to the police and charge you with assault."

"Nah." Steve finally looked at David. "She wouldn't go to the police. But why are you talking assault?"

"Mitch," put in Veronica, before David could say more. She feared David and Steve would brawl here and now because Steve, unlike Mitch, did not seem the type to back down. And David wouldn't care if his opponent was bigger than he was. Or used knives. Her hand came to rest on her side.

"Mitch is full of shit, which I'm sure you observed after spending two minutes with him." Steve's smile was weirdly charming, yet cold. "He paints a bad picture of me because he's jealous." He jabbed a thumb at David. "As is this guy, right?"

"Why are you here?" she asked.

"Old times."

"Since I don't remember old times, that's meaningless to me."

His gray, flat gaze met hers, unblinking. "Did the FBI find

you?"

She stiffened and her heart began to bang against her ribs in protest. Her body wanted to run.

His lips curled in satisfaction, pleased he'd scared her. "They were very interested in you. But I couldn't tell them a thing because, poof, you were gone. You didn't even leave footprints in the snow. By the way, agent Walters was inordinately interested in the wolves, just like you. FBI and wolves. Who knew?"

Don't panic. Don't panic.

"What the hell do you want?" demanded David.

"I wanted to say hello. I didn't know you'd all be frightened and I'd be left standing outdoors behind a locked screen door."

David scowled. "You're not welcome here, Steve. That's why you're standing outside."

Steve shifted his gaze. "How are you doing, Linc?"

Linc had been hanging back, taking everything in. "Fine." He tried to sound careless.

"How do you know my nephew's name?" David's voice was low and intense.

"We chatted before you got here." Steve smirked.

"You didn't have much time."

"Sure we did. We exchanged names."

"Linc?" David cast a glance back.

"Yeah. We exchanged names," Linc parroted unconvincingly.

"Well," observed Steve. "This guy's more protective than Mitch, isn't he? But maybe we'll meet again, Veronica."

"I don't think so," said David.

Steve lifted a hand in goodbye, then turned to leave.

"Hold it." David reached the screen door and unlocked it, pushed it open. "How do you know Linc?"

Steve stopped on the steps. "I'm a friend of a friend of his father's."

"Who's the friend?"

"Henry LeBlanc."

Linc blanched.

"I'm Henry's messenger boy. A reminder," Steve explained. "Linc knows him."

"No," denied Linc hoarsely.

Steve started to walk away.

"Wait," commanded David, which amused Steve. "Call the police," David hissed at Linc, then followed Steve out.

Veronica's heart was in her throat. She knew in her bones Steve was dangerous. She followed to back David up.

"Who the fuck are you?" David stalked after Steve. "Making these stupid cryptic remarks just for the thrill of scaring teenage boys."

Steve responded by pulling out a knife and twisting it in the moonlight, causing David to stop short with a jerk. Veronica's chest went tight with fear.

"I have no intention of hurting anyone. Unless I'm attacked." Steve's overly reasonable tone made the situation worse. Because the knife wasn't reasonable.

"David," breathed Veronica. Knife or no, she was scared he'd go after Steve.

"Get back," David told her.

She couldn't leave him. Rather, she grabbed his arm so he wouldn't follow Steve who had backed up to his station wagon. When he jumped inside and started the engine, Veronica found that her lungs began to work again.

David swore viciously as the car peeled out of the driveway and down the road. This was the station wagon they'd seen over a week ago when she'd chased Steve off the property. She wondered if David recognized the vehicle.

"No license." He marched back up the stairs. "Call the police, Linc. *Now.*"

"He's just a jerk." Despite the stubborn set to his mouth, Linc's voice trembled. Veronica wondered what hold Steve had on Linc. For that matter, what hold did Steve have on her? It was hard to know when you're memory-impaired. FBI? Whatever had she done in her past?

David grabbed the phone but before he dialed, he asked Linc, "Do you know this man Steve?"

"No."

"Have you ever met him before?"

"No."

"Who is Henry LeBlanc?"

Linc didn't say anything and appeared to be mustering defiance.

"*Answer me.*"

"I dunno," Linc mumbled.

"You're lying." Looking tired, David dialed in to report the incident to whoever was on the other end of the phone.

Linc moved to leave and David put up a hand. "You stay here."

The boy slumped, but obeyed. Veronica wasn't surprised. David was fuming.

When David hung up, Linc said, his voice too high, "Henry LeBlanc is a colleague of my father's. It means nothing."

"Messenger boy? Reminder?" David asked. "Our pal Steve thought the name meant something."

Linc shrugged defiantly.

"Should I phone Aaron to find out?"

"If you want."

David pinched the bridge of his nose and picked up the phone again. But instead of dialing, he stared at Veronica. "And you. FBI? What the hell is that about? I thought Mitch was bullshitting because why would the FBI be in Canada? Are you American?"

"I don't know." Veronica echoed Linc's position, aware she was as much, if not more, of a burden than Linc.

David's expression sharpened and he slowly put the phone back on its cradle. He'd made some kind of decision. "Look, Veronica, you need to disappear. I just don't think we can explain your presence right now. Nor do you remember Steve, so you won't be able to shed any light on this incident." He addressed Linc. "Don't mention Veronica to the police."

"Why not?"

"Because." David looked at a loss, then soldiered on. "Veronica's ex-husband is stalking her and he'll find her if she turns up in tonight's police report." He winced at his story but Linc didn't notice.

"Really?" Linc gaped at Veronica as if she were a celebrity.

"You don't want to talk to the police, I don't think," David muttered to her, taking her aside. "Are you okay?"

She nodded, though her limbs were shaking.

"They'll be here soon. You have no ID, no last name and no memory. Not only will they be inordinately interested in you, it will distract them from Linc's situation. And I'm more convinced than ever that he has a situation. This way we can deal with one thing at a time." He didn't even mention the real problem—Veronica was a shapeshifter.

"Okay." But she didn't want to leave them. Linc and David were her pack.

"Meet me in the tent when everything settles down. You'll know when the police are gone, right?"

"I'll know." On impulse, she kissed his cheek, lips brushing stubble, then walked away. The woods would take her in.

∽

While Nell talked calmly on the phone, David stared straight ahead. He could hear Aaron yelling through the wire and he wanted to rip the phone out of Nell's hand and tear a strip off his erstwhile brother-in-law. Self-centered bastard who couldn't understand why his ex-wife's family had to keep bugging him since *he* didn't have custody of Linc.

No wonder Linc had disappeared upstairs.

"Did you have to phone the police *again?*" asked his mother, as if David was inflicting his bad habit on innocents. Nell glanced at her mother and left the room.

"I felt it best, yes." David's words came out rather strangled.

"You need to use judgment in these situations."

"I judged." Some asshole had pulled a knife on him for Chrissakes, with Linc and Veronica nearby.

"And was phoning Aaron for the best?" continued his mother. "It warms my heart to hear him yell at my daughter. Hasn't Nell been through enough without your help?"

David resumed staring straight ahead, unseeing.

"And you say Veronica is out?"

He rubbed his forehead. "I did say that." Veronica, he thought in despair. FBI, amnesia, *werewolf*. He didn't know how to handle her problems. There were too many of them. And there was Linc.

David decided to steer the conversation elsewhere. "The police say that a Steve MacKinnon—who fits this man's description—has caused problems in the past."

"By breaking trapping laws," said his mother. "Not anything to do with Linc and banks."

"This guy seems to have a varied and shady past. Which is why the police want to be informed."

"Mom." Nell walked back into the room, her face drawn. David wished he could have spared her all this worry. "David was right to call the police. They're looking for this Steve MacKinnon now. They want to talk to him."

"Well, they can settle it then," said Mom.

"If they find him, which is the problem," David pointed out. "He moves around and he's not always easy to track down."

"He pulled a knife on you?" his mother asked for the third time, just as incredulous as before.

"Yes. As you heard me tell the police." He shifted to look at Nell. "Fun conversation with Aaron?"

"No. I loathe the man." She looked around the room. "Hey, in all the excitement I lost track of your friend Veronica. Where is she?"

"Out." His mother's tone suggested Veronica's absence was responsible for the upheaval.

"Okay," said Nell slowly. "So she missed the fun?"

"Yes." David felt guilty about the lie, especially when Veronica was connected to Steve. And the nature of that connection was a complete mystery to him. He hoped keeping Veronica's existence from the police wouldn't prove to be a grave mistake. It made sense an hour ago when Veronica had stood beside him, vulnerable and innocent. Now it made him uneasy.

But she had to be innocent. David couldn't be that far off the mark. If only he had a history of reading women well. Unfortunately, most of his girlfriends had accused him of understanding nothing about them.

"What does Aaron say about Henry LeBlanc?" David asked Nell.

"LeBlanc is Aaron's boss. A good, upstanding citizen who doesn't deserve to be pulled into Linc's stupid games. We—that's you and I, David—should stop being so gullible and paranoid."

David snorted. "Gullible *and* paranoid, that's an interesting combination."

"I thought so. I should try it some time. But right now, I just feel worried."

"Where is Linc?" asked Mom.

"Flamequest," pronounced Nell in a voice of doom.

"You shouldn't let him play that game quite so much," said their mother disapprovingly. "A little bit is fine, but he goes overboard."

"Thanks, Mom, for the advice. But I'm not going to make his game my priority tonight."

"Well." Mom looked offended. "I had better push off. Too much excitement around here for me." At the look on Nell's face, she faltered. "Oh honey, surely it's not serious."

"I don't know. I'm thinking it might be."

"Things will look better in the morning. They always do."

Nell nodded weakly.

"Get some rest tonight. You have David to watch over you."

"Lucky him."

"That's fine, Nell," David assured her.

"David likes camping," Mom added brightly.

Nell rolled her eyes. "In the wilderness, Mom, not in my backyard."

"I'm sure David doesn't mind."

"David doesn't mind," he agreed. "Now scoot, Mom. It's past your bedtime. I should know. I'm the watch."

She regarded him for a moment and David feared she was going to say something like, *You're a good boy*, but she just nodded and turned to go.

He and Nell watched their mother leave, then retreated to the living room.

Nell flopped down in a chair. "I'm exhausted and I haven't even yelled at Linc yet." She glanced at her watch. "Maybe in ten minutes."

"Yeah," said David. "It's good to see him step up to the plate and take responsibility by playing his computer game."

She grimaced. "He's young. Too young."

"He's also genuinely frightened."

"What did the police tell Linc this time?"

"Nothing much. They grilled him and his *I don't knows* became frantic." David thought of Veronica and felt guilty again. He was certainly not modeling tell-all behavior tonight.

"Well, if he's been lying and telling stories since this mess started then he wouldn't know anything." She entertained this possibility with some hope.

David shook his head. "Why would Steve MacKinnon say

he's Henry LeBlanc's messenger boy? Linc didn't make that up. I heard it."

"According to my ex, Henry isn't impressed that Linc stole Aaron's password."

"Who is?"

Her shoulders slumped. "I suppose there must be something to it if this Steve guy came to my doorstep."

"Yes." David thought of Steve with his knife and Veronica's ribs.

Nell rubbed her eyes with the heels of her hands. "I'm going to hit the sack and sleep. If I can." Her red eyes met his.

"Okay. Lock everything up and yell if you need me."

Nell rose and hugged him. Unusual. They weren't a demonstrative family. "Thanks for being here."

"Sure." He knew he sounded stiff.

Nell let out a laugh. "I love you, too, David."

The doorbell rang, interrupting their exchange. They stared at each other. Then David walked to the front.

"It's me," Bob called through the locked door.

David gestured to Nell who passed him by, letting Bob in.

"Hi, David," said Bob cheerfully.

"Good night." At David's flat tone, Bob frowned in consternation. Well, Nell could explain. Even if Bob annoyed David, he was another body in the house. Someone who could set off an alarm if Steve MacKinnon returned.

Chapter Twelve

As Nell and Bob headed upstairs, David stood in the unlit kitchen, allowing his eyes to adjust to the dark. The evening had been a mess, if not a disaster, and there was still Veronica to deal with.

He didn't believe she had anything to do with Steve threatening Linc. But he had made Linc and himself erase Veronica's presence from their narration of Steve MacKinnon's visit. When he knew so little about her. And this bothered him.

His gut feeling, when she was around, said she was a good person who needed help. He wished he could make sense of the fact that Steve seemed to know both Veronica and Linc.

He blew out a gust of air and moved, locking the door behind him as he left the house. Before now his ability to judge women had never mattered. He'd picked himself up from one or the other deteriorating relationship and moved on. Often with relief.

Veronica was different. He couldn't abandon her. Nor could he hand her over to the police or the FBI or Steve. She trusted him. Yet he had to place Linc first and he didn't quite know how to do that. Unless he asked Veronica to leave.

"Hi."

He jumped. She'd stolen up beside him, unnoticed despite the back porch light shining on the yard. Quiet as a creature of the night—which she was—her eyes shone moonlight. In all sorts of ways he was in way over his head.

He stopped at the tent.

"How'd it go?" When he didn't say anything, she added, "With the police."

"We didn't mention you."

She blinked at his curt answer. "Thanks. I guess I'm hard to explain."

When he didn't respond to her tentative smile, she looked down. "How's Linc?"

"Same."

Her brow furrowed. "Are you okay?"

"I'm tired." He slapped the mosquito on his neck. Telling her to leave was a lot easier in theory than in practice. She just seemed so eager to be with him. But something of his thoughts must have come through.

"I see." She swallowed.

"You don't know Steve at all and don't remember him, right?"

She looked straight at him. "I remember his smell."

"His *smell*? From last year?" She was pulling his leg. She had to be.

"From last week. Didn't you recognize his station wagon? He's the one I chased through the forest with you following us. He's the one I smelled."

It made less and less sense. "How does Steve know Linc?" David slapped at another mosquito. "I'm getting eaten alive here. It's time to hit the sack."

She eyed him, waiting for an invitation.

Maybe you should go was on the tip of his tongue, but it

sounded cowardly. "I'm concerned about this connection you have with Steve," he ground out. "Are you hiding something?"

"There's not much to hide, David. You know that. You know everything about me that I know."

He slapped again while she stood still. "What? Do werewolves not get bitten by insects?"

"The bites don't bother me," she said tonelessly.

He shut his eyes. "I didn't like lying to the police, telling them only Linc and I were here tonight."

"I'm sorry."

"I don't know what to do with you."

"You don't have to do anything. You must know that. I can leave. That's what you want, isn't it?"

"I wish," he muttered and she shrank from him. "Look," he said more loudly, while she mumbled, "I'll go."

He grabbed her hand. It was trembling. He did not have to choose between Linc and Veronica. It was a false dichotomy. They were both innocents. Nothing pointed towards Veronica.

He pulled her to him. "Let's sleep on it, first. Get in the tent. I need to go back inside and grab an extra blanket for you."

"You trust me?"

David made a noise of frustration. "It's not about trust. It's about doing the right thing."

"Uh-huh." She didn't sound convinced.

"Give me a few minutes." He jogged inside, ducked into the bathroom, then stole a blanket from Nell's linen closet. As he left the house, the mosquitoes found him again. He reached the tent, zipped open the door as quickly as possible and clambered in, hoping to leave the insects outside.

"Veronica? Here's a blanket. It can get chilly at night."

She reached for it. Just that action made his heart beat fast. He wished things were simple between them. His body wanted simple.

"I locked the house." He needed to keep to the mundane, and ignore the blood rushing south. Because with Veronica's past, lovemaking complicated matters further. He did not feel equipped to deal with her fears tonight. It was obvious she'd been roughly handled in the past. She had scars to prove it. And what her mind did not remember, her body did.

"I have exceptional hearing. I'll know if the house has visitors, if that's any comfort to you."

"Good." He was aware he sounded fervent. "This Steve visit has me on edge," he felt compelled to explain.

"And angry."

"Well, yeah. I didn't appreciate his stunt with the knife. Or his getting off on scaring you and Linc."

"I was worried you'd go after him when he held the knife."

"I'm not stupid."

"Just brave." Her words were sincere and admiring, an embarrassing combination.

"Not particularly brave."

"You're brave to be with me, David," she whispered and he was undone.

"No." It was too complicated to say more. They sat there in awkward silence. He caught her ankle and shook it slightly. "Why do you say that?"

"I think..." She laughed a little. "What do I know, eh? My memory is gone. But I *suspect* that men are usually frightened of werewolves."

"I met you as wolf first." He released her ankle. The tent

was too small for both of them, he couldn't boot her out, and he couldn't send her into the house. He didn't know what to do.

"I'm pretty sure Mitch didn't know what I was. Thank God."

"Mitch is an idiot."

"Don't ask me how I ended up with him, because I can't tell you. I can't tell you about Steve, either, and that makes you angry."

"I'm not angry *at you*, Veronica."

"I'm scared Steve knows." Her voice shook with emotion. "He was talking about wolves."

"Because you reacted." Despite himself, he slid a hand up her calf. "He's one of those people who likes to frighten others. It makes him feel important. I hope the police pick him up and arrest him."

She sat forward and he realized she was nude. "The knife scared me."

He reached for her scored side, touching the scars gently.

"Why would he knife me?" she asked. "Because I wouldn't sleep with him?"

"Oh, babe, I don't know."

She came forward then, wrapping her arms around his neck, and kissed him full on the mouth. He responded to the hum of her skin, the urgency underneath, and the kiss went long and deep. She broke off to pull his shirt over his head and explore his skin with her mouth, teeth and tongue. Her touch was expert, his body sang in reaction, and yet he could feel her speed up when he needed them to slow down. He touched her arms, the scars, the long, narrow spine that ran down her back.

"So beautiful," he murmured. A weight lifted off him as she became his total focus. He pulled her to him so he could kiss her mouth again, the intimacy entrancing him with her sweet taste and her eagerness. Joy even. They sat chest to chest, tongues entwined. One hand captured her lovely breast.

He tried to keep her there at foreplay and touch, where she didn't tense up with fear, but the pressure was building, and not just within her. Still, her pliant body could, he knew from past experience, stiffen to shatter. He wanted soft and slow, and he didn't want their mutual need to break the spell they'd woven.

She pushed against him, depriving him of her touch while she pulled his boxers down. As he shifted to help her, the seductive haze was broken by David's memory of the other time they had gotten naked together, when they had moved too quickly.

He caught her wrists in one hand.

"What?" she demanded a little wildly.

"What are you doing?"

"What do you mean?"

"Why so fast?"

"This is fast?" Her bewilderment added tension to her body and he worked to ease it, skimming a hand over her side and back, lightly running a palm over the cleft of her buttocks to see if that calmed or unnerved her.

She seemed to be at a loss for words. With her wrists still trapped, he leaned forward and kissed her, closed-mouth, tender. She began to pant.

"Hey." He released her and pulled her into a hug. She liked hugs and kisses. He knew that. Maybe this was where they should begin and end. He hoped to manage that without too much frustration.

She was shivering in his arms. "I want to make love with you," she said through gritted teeth.

A part of him was gratified by her intensity. But he needed the sex to finish well.

She pushed at him. "*David.*"

He rested a hand on the inside of her thigh and she looked down at it. His fingers brushed the fold between her thigh and pubis, stroking closer. She jumped when he touched her clit.

"Yes," she said, but faltering.

"Okay, but let's wait until you're wet." With some relief he understood kissing and hugging was not going to be enough for Veronica either.

He kept his fingers there, circling the sensitive skin, coming back to her clit, and she gasped.

"Should I stop?" he asked.

"No."

He leaned her back and trailed kisses down her neck and breast until he caught her nipple between his teeth. She jumped again. He kissed the nipple in apology, then spoke. "No?"

"Yes." She was panting, but not the tense, tight pants of earlier.

He continued.

"It's just, David," she began.

He made an encouraging sound.

"I'd forgotten," she blurted.

He stopped teasing the nipple but didn't remove his fingers from her sex. She was softening under his touch, getting ready to ride his hand.

He leaned his forehead against hers. "What did you forget?"

"What this is like."

"Tell me," he murmured.

"The heat, spreading outwards, the, uh, feeling hazy good. Do you know what I mean?"

"Maybe," he teased.

"I can't explain. Especially right now." She arched and moaned. An orgasm, perhaps, but not an intense one. Still, that was good, very good.

She came back to him. "I've missed it." She kissed him hungrily, some of her desperation coming back, but not out of control. He was more comfortable with her, too. He no longer feared he would lose her along the way. Her hands roamed his skin, exploring with less urgency and more wonder.

She gripped his cock, one thumb circling the glans expertly and he almost said, *You've done this before*, then censored himself. There was open and there was too complicated for the moment.

She broke away, smiling. "You're wet."

"Uh, yeah." With the pressure building again, he didn't know how well he was going to control this wave.

"I was worried you didn't want me."

"That is not something you have to worry about."

He reached for a condom. As he ripped open the package, she stared down, biting her lip as he rolled it on.

"I'd forgotten this, too."

"So I gathered. But you've remembered a few things," he added appreciatively.

She looked pleased.

He caught her chin in his hand. "Are you ready?"

She pushed him down and climbed on top. He hadn't actually wanted the same position as last time, but perhaps she was most comfortable this way. At least he would be able to hold on past entry tonight.

She slid down his length and he groaned, no longer able to think about anything except this connection. Placing her feet on either side of his thighs, she settled into a crouch. She rode him, hard and fast, overwhelming everything but the rising need of his cock. Her hands pressed down on his chest and she breathed quickly, too quickly. He broke the enchantment by pulling her down to him so she lay on his chest.

"What are you doing?" she asked.

He nibbled her earlobe. "You're wonderful."

"Then why did you stop me?"

"Just a coffee break."

She laughed, the note a little high. "I don't understand."

"Did you like that?"

"I like not thinking," she admitted. She kissed his shoulder. "Is that bad? Did you like it?"

"No. Yes."

"Oh good," she said with clear relief. "I thought I'd had it wrong."

"No." He was emphatic. "There are many rights. I thought I'd try another."

They kissed for quite some time. He moved beneath her, kissing her, one hand on her nape so she couldn't get away. The lovemaking was slow and languorous, exactly how he wanted it. An appreciation. Then the tension built and she pushed up again.

His hands on her hips, she let him position her so he went deeper. She moved again, hard and swift, and he held on until she shuddered. He swore as he came, joining her and she kept moving, drawing out their pleasure until he could no longer stand it and he stilled her.

"Shit," she said, wide-eyed, still sitting up. "I don't

remember that."

Before she could move away, he gathered her to him,
rocking her, running a hand up and down her backside.

She clung. It took him a minute to realize his neck felt
damp. Some of his doubts returned.

"Veronica?" he murmured.

She nodded against him.

"You okay?"

"Yes."

He didn't know what he wanted her to say, but something.
It had been years since he'd been this emotionally involved with
a woman and he barely knew her. She barely knew herself.

"You were wonderful," he said.

"I bet you say that to all the girls."

"No." He rolled on to his side, taking her with him, and he
kissed her salty lips. "What girls are you talking about?"

"I dunno."

"There's only you now."

She nodded but looked uncertain. "David?"

"Yes?"

"Can I sleep with you all night?"

He felt like she'd punched him. How could she ask when
he'd just loved her as best he could? With the pad of his thumb,
he wiped away the moisture from the corner of her eye. "Do you
expect me to turn you out now?"

She didn't move, just stared, and he shook his head. Not
that sex changed everything, but he had passed beyond the
moment when he could tell her to leave. If that moment had
ever existed.

He pulled a blanket over them both and after a slight

pause, she nestled up against him, head on his shoulder.

"I like to breathe you in," she said, as if admitting to a big secret. He kissed her hair.

They still had much to talk about, but that would have to be part of future conversations. Worried she would sneak off, he waited until her breathing became deep and regular before falling asleep himself.

Some time later, he came awake, aware of Veronica in his arms, her back against his chest now, her breathing fast if not panicked, her body moving in small jerks. Dreaming. Tense.

"Shhh." He stroked her unruly hair and hooked his arm around her waist, pulling her closer. "You're okay." He felt her calm under his touch.

She settled against him without seeming to wake, her body relaxing into his, her heart rate returning to its low and steady rate. He listened in the darkness and heard only the insect noises of summer. At this moment, everyone was safe.

ℰℭ

She woke abruptly, as she always did. But the sleep itself had been deeper and longer than any she could remember. It was as if she rose from some great, calming depth, revitalized.

No intruders had been at the house, she was sure of it, because the wrong kind of noise would have punctured sleep and brought her awake. Besides, she smelt safety. Felt it, too, with David's hand on her stomach and his breath on her neck.

She'd dreamt of her brother again. That usually upset her. But this dream had been different. Instead of an angry, frightened teen, he'd been older and smiling. She hadn't seen him smile before. Maybe he was happy for her, that she'd found someone who cared about her. Fanciful, to think the dream brother more than her own creation cobbled from a broken memory, and able to feel on his own, but she played with that idea.

Because, despite her lack of memory, she missed him.

"Good morning."

She turned in David's arms, eager to see his face, yet wondering, too, what the morning would bring. Last night, after Steve's visit, though he hadn't voiced his concerns, David had been suspicious of her.

He smiled and kissed her forehead. Her fears fled.

"Oh." She brushed against his erection.

"You'd forgotten that, too?"

"Uh."

"How good is your hearing?"

"Pretty damn good."

"For example, is anyone in the house up?"

"No."

"Don't move." He reached for a condom, took care of himself and nudged her apart with his knee.

"Do you like mornings?" He waited just outside her.

"I do now."

He parted her and she welcomed him, still languorous from the night before. No time for worries or concerns to build. She'd been anxious about pleasing him last night, in case he wouldn't have her back.

"You're lovely." He paced himself, the rhythm neither fast nor slow and she edged down, wanting to get closer. "Yes." He became more focused. She wrapped her legs around him and rose to meet him.

"Do you like this?" he asked.

"Yes," she said fiercely. "Do you always talk when you make love?"

"Just to you. You're special."

She kissed him, joining him. The heat spread through her body.

"Come on," he whispered.

"What?"

He moved faster, harder, his kisses became more urgent. It excited her, this new David, who wanted as much as she did.

She exploded, thought fleeing, as he pumped into her, groaning. And then she buried her face into his neck, to keep him close and hold onto the moment. She warned herself not to cry again. Last night the tears had been acceptable, but not in the harsh light of day. She had to keep her emotions in check.

They lay together, catching their breath. Then he began to move away.

"Stay in me. I like you here."

He smiled. "I like it, too, but I have to take care of the condom."

She didn't think they needed the condom, but couldn't come up with a decent rationale why not, so she kept quiet as he sat up. While he disposed of it, she snuggled up to his back and gave his shoulders small kisses.

"I could get used to this."

"Yeah?" She wasn't quite sure what. The sex, she assumed.

He turned and traced her mouth with his thumb. "I haven't had such an affectionate lover before."

This pleased her inordinately. She was special.

"At least when you're not dead set on having intercourse

right away. Like the first time." He cocked his head, his face gently inquiring. "What was that about?"

The question was so nonjudgmental, she didn't mind answering. "It's just what I know."

"I mean." He looked away, as if he were embarrassed. "It can be good that way, if you're ready. But sometimes when you're getting to know someone, slow can..." He rubbed the back of his neck, laughing ruefully. "I don't usually talk about sex. I just do it."

"Oh, it's interesting."

He gave a bark of laughter. "I wouldn't talk sex simply to be interesting. Especially when I don't know how to. But it's important, given your lack of memory, you know? To make some things clear?"

Despite his evident concern for her, his face had heated up. She stroked his cheek. "I was nervous last night." She didn't add that she thought it was do or die, that he would get rid of her if she didn't somehow bind him to her. It sounded all wrong and she wasn't sure what to do with her feelings of desperation. She set them aside. "Sorry," she added, though he wouldn't understand why she was apologizing.

"No sorrys. This is just about being clear."

She nodded guiltily.

"But as far as I'm concerned that's enough clarity for now. Small doses and all that."

They dressed quietly and exited the tent after a last embrace. It was early and the grass was damp. Moisture clung to her feet as they walked to the house.

"Can I make pancakes?" After watching Eleanor at the stove, Veronica was confident she remembered how to make them.

"Sure." Once in the kitchen, David pulled out the different ingredients and a pan. "I'm going to have a shower, okay?"

"Okay."

His arm came around her and he kissed her cheek. Then he was gone.

She got to work cracking eggs. The shower started overhead and Linc stole downstairs, as if he'd deliberately avoided David.

"You're up early," she said brightly and he looked taken aback. She realized she felt great and tried to dim her smile.

Because Linc did not look great. He slouched into a chair. His eyes were hollow and troubled. "Veronica, can I ask you a question?"

"Yes."

"How do you know that Steve guy?"

She turned away quickly. Well, that was one way to douse her ebullience. She tried to adopt a casual tone. "I don't. How do you know him?"

Linc didn't answer and she saw he was fiddling with the napkin holder. He looked at her, defiant. "I don't know him either, then."

She couldn't confide in Linc unless she told him she had amnesia and she wasn't up for that. *I might have lived with him,* seemed impossible to say, particularly when she couldn't fathom living with a man like Steve MacKinnon.

"Last night you told us that you'd never met him before," she said slowly.

"Oh, I haven't." He looked over his shoulder to see who was coming down the hall towards them.

Veronica smelled Bob before he came into sight. "Morning all."

Linc scowled.

"I'm Bob. You must be Veronica." He extended his hand. Veronica wiped hers on a dish towel and they shook.

"Good morning," she responded politely, since he was beaming at her.

"I've heard a lot about you."

"From who?" demanded Linc, as if it was his duty to defend her honor.

Bob's good-morning cheer lessened. "Aren't you usually in bed till noon?"

"Not when someone wakes me up."

Bob flushed and Veronica returned to her work. "I'm making pancakes," she found herself chirping.

"Any coffee?" Bob looked at Veronica expectantly, but she didn't know how to make coffee.

"Call Mom down," said Linc. "I'm sure she'll scurry around the kitchen making you some."

"Linc." A freshly damp David, who'd just had the fastest shower in history, strode into the kitchen. "Mind your manners. *I* will scurry around and make you coffee, Bob, how about that?"

Linc glowered while Bob expressed his gratitude.

"No problem," David assured him while Veronica frowned into the batter. She hadn't thought David liked Bob.

"Actually, Bob, I wanted to ask you a question." David stood, coffee can in hand. "Otherwise I wouldn't scurry."

"It's my lucky morning, then. Shoot."

"You've heard of Steve MacKinnon."

Veronica found it hard to concentrate on what she was doing so she turned and stared at the two men.

"Unfortunately, yes."

"Thank God someone will admit to knowing the man." David cast Linc a glance.

Linc slammed the metal napkin holder onto the table and stomped out of the room.

Bob blinked. "What was that about?"

David sighed. "Never mind. Tell me about Steve MacKinnon."

"He's bad news."

"I was hoping for something more specific."

Bob leaned back. "Well, I've heard of him because he traps wolves illegally. You know, out of season, inside park boundaries. Sneaky bastard, he's hard to catch red-handed. He's smart and he knows the land well."

Veronica felt like throwing up. Noise roared in her ears and it was all she could do to breathe. The trap had been Steve's. She was sure of it. The smell of danger had lingered with her ever since that evening her paw had been crushed.

She turned and focused on beating the eggs, barely able to follow the rest of the conversation.

"Is this about the wolf you found last winter?" asked Bob.

"No. It's about Linc. Steve MacKinnon appears to know Linc."

"That boy causes Nell too much grief." Bob's voice was heavy with disapproval.

"Yeah, well, if you ever decide to pay Linc any attention, it might help Nell out."

"The boy isn't civil to me."

"The boy's name is Linc. And he's in trouble. Where does Steve live now? I've got an out-of-date address."

"I have no idea. You and Linc don't want to know either.

He's dirty. People find out where he lives when they want something stolen, or someone to get hurt."

Like her. Like Linc.

"I need to talk to him," David insisted.

"I can't help you. The police would have a better idea."

"They're looking."

"Well, leave them to it."

"Thanks for the advice," said David insincerely.

Veronica shivered. David was determined to see this through, because of her, or because of Linc. In that moment, she knew she would have to meet Steve MacKinnon again. If only to protect her pack.

Chapter Thirteen

The day was blessedly quiet, a relief after last night's excitement with its impromptu visit by a knife-wielding man who claimed to know her. Veronica enjoyed having only Linc and David at the house. Nell was working and Eleanor didn't drop by.

Though Linc was difficult. He came downstairs to eat. She and David joined him at the kitchen table, but he only toyed with his food.

"There a problem?" demanded David as Linc drummed his fork on the table and ignored his syrup-soaked pancake.

"What?" Startled, Linc jerked his head up.

David looked pointedly at the fork and Linc's hand stilled.

"*No*," said Linc, as if David had asked the stupidest question ever.

"Good. Why don't you eat then?"

"What's with you?" Linc almost shouted and marched back upstairs.

Veronica had never seen him like this, rude and restless. David turned to her, eyebrows raised. "What did I say?"

"Maybe he's upset about last night's visit." She still was.

So David made his way to Linc's bedroom and suggested the three of them go to McMasters that evening for dinner.

Veronica gathered from David that Linc should consider this a treat. Even so, Linc kept away from them, hanging out in his room and stomping around an awful lot. David taught her card games and they tried to ignore the boy's noise.

She decided they were out of milk—because during his next sortie, Linc asked where it had all gone—so she offered to walk to the corner store to restock the supply. David stayed at the house with Linc while she took her time, enjoying the hot, sunny day with its mild breeze, sun and wind on her love-touched skin. Despite concerns about Linc and Steve, she was happy.

After her return, distracted by her happiness and by David, it took her almost ten minutes to realize it was very quiet upstairs.

She looked at David as he counted up his crib.

"What?"

"Where's Linc?" She should have noted the silence earlier.

He pointed to the ceiling.

"I don't hear him."

"That's because he's no longer stomping and is now glued to the computer." David paused, tension building. "Isn't it?"

"It seems too quiet."

David strode to the bottom of the stairs. "Linc," he called, hand on the banister. He turned to Veronica. "I've always wondered why Nell didn't just go to his room rather than yell from down here. But I'm beginning to see how tiresome it is to tramp up and down the stairs when he should have heard you the first time. *Linc!*" he roared and Veronica's heart sank.

David saw her face and ran up, taking two stairs at a time. Veronica heard four different doors open and shut before David, now white-faced, leapt back down.

"You're right. He's not there."

They raced around the rest of the house and the yard, looking for Linc, calling his name.

"Why would he disappear?" David demanded, as if Veronica had the answer.

"I don't know."

"Hell. He snuck out on me. Why would he sneak out on me? Where would he go?"

"I don't know." But she caught a whiff of Linc at that moment and focused on his scent in the front yard.

"But we're going to McMasters. He *loves* McMasters. I thought it would cheer him up." David turned as if to run around to the back again and Veronica put a hand on his arm.

"Wait." She crouched down to wolf level and breathed in deeply. Closer to the ground, Linc's scent was stronger. She moved to confirm her senses, then stopped.

"Linc's gone that way." She pointed to the road leading away from town.

"What are you talking about?" David stared down at her. "How do you know where he's gone?"

She tipped her head up at him, her mouth curved slightly. "I'm wolf, remember? Linc's left a trail."

David blinked, taking a moment to process that piece of information. "Okay. How long ago did he leave?"

"Not long, I don't think." It wasn't like she was an expert tracker. She had little experience, that she remembered. Besides this nose—human—was all wrong for tracking. It was difficult to tease out the different scents and they were all so faint. She pushed herself up to standing. "When did you last talk to him?"

"An hour ago, just after you went out. He told me he was

going to have a nap."

"He probably left shortly afterwards."

David's fist jerked up in an angry gesture. "I can't believe he'd pull this kind of stupid-ass stunt."

"Maybe he felt he had to."

David rounded on her. "Why? I've been here since the aborted camping trip. I've tried everything to get him to confide in me, yet it's all been tears and recriminations and sulky silences."

She shrugged helplessly.

"I believed in him and he still sneaks out on me. How can I help him when he lies to me? I'm ready to wring his neck." His intense gaze was unsettling. "Please don't lie to me, Veronica. Even by omission."

"I won't." She knew he wasn't talking about her unprofessed fear of abandonment. "You know everything about my past that I do, David."

He bowed his head for a moment, then took a deep breath. "Okay, let's get in the car."

"I can't track him in the car," she pointed out.

"*Track* him?"

"Yes."

His expression wasn't incredulous, more nonplussed.

"In fact, I had better do this properly and shift. To wolf."

Now he looked wary, as if she were pulling his leg. They'd communicated well last night, when it had been physical, but this conversation was difficult.

"Yeah?" was all he said.

She nodded. "It takes me ten or fifteen minutes to recover from the shift."

"Recover?" He whipped his head back and forth in frustration. "I can't wait. I don't know what the hell Linc is up to."

"It's because the shift uses up a bit of energy," she added, trying to keep to practicalities.

"I see." He ran a hand through his hair. "Okay look, I'm going to jump in the car and search for Linc while you, uh, shift. Nell is going to freak if she gets home to find Linc is missing. Because at long last I've convinced her this is serious. Or maybe Steve's visit did that for me."

Veronica felt chilled thinking about that man. She needed to find Linc, and fast. As she turned to leave, David grabbed her by the shoulders and kissed her hard. "Don't hurt yourself," he warned.

"I've shifted before."

"I sometimes forget." Despite his fears for Linc, he managed a quirky, rueful smile, and Veronica felt better. "I'll be back as soon as I can," he called over his shoulder as he jogged to his car.

She ran the other way, to the woods beyond the backyard. It was late afternoon, the moon was not yet in the sky, and her body did not want to shift, especially after a night of making love with David. Her resistance surprised her. Until recently, wolf had been her default form, and now she wanted to stay human and stay with her lover.

Concern for Linc's well-being pushed her to be otherwise. She stripped, crouched low and breathed slowly, focusing inward, to where the change began. For the first time, she found herself bracing against the pain that came with the rearrangement of bone and muscle.

That took her aback. She paused and had to start again. Before now the pain had been a strange kind of punishing relief, a place where she didn't have to think. She tried to embrace it yet again, as she always had, but that didn't work. So she turned outwards, breathing in damp woods and green leaves, thinking of forest life. *Be what you need to be.*

The dizziness that presaged the shift overtook her with a force she wasn't accustomed to. She fell, letting go of thought and humanity. Her body turned away from her mind and she lost all sense of herself.

She woke on her side, panting, disoriented. The world was new and strange. Tasting the air she caught man-smell and pollution in the forest's smells. What had she been thinking to shift so close to houses? Risky and she was old enough to know better. Then, from the pile of clothing that lay near her, she recognized a man's scent—*David*. His scent mingled with hers and her location no longer seemed dangerous.

Linc. The day's memories jumbled back in.

Gingerly, she rose on all fours, feeling alien in her familiar wolf skin. The forest's smell overwhelmed her with pine and squirrel and wildflower. And David again. But it was Linc she had to find and he wasn't here. She looked around and saw the sky was darker than it had been before the shift. How long had she lain here? The moon's absence and her body's desire to stay human had made the process more draining than usual.

Yet adrenaline did its work and she trotted out of the woods and around to the front of the house, hyper-aware of her surroundings, given the real possibility that strangers would suddenly appear in this suburb.

David was gone. His trail ended where the car had been, his distinctive musk obliterated by gasoline. But Linc's trail, though fainter, still led away from town. She began to lope, following his scent. If they were lucky, David had already found Linc and all was well.

She had little confidence in that scenario. In her world, things didn't work out. They got more complicated and painful. She shoved that thought away.

The traffic was minimal. The road turned to gravel half a mile on and she moved swiftly, picking up speed until she heard a car approaching. She ducked into the bushes beside the road and waited till it passed, then returned to the road.

When a second car came along, she hid again. This time a station wagon whipped by and she recognized it by sight. She crouched there, frozen by the knowledge that the car belonged to Steve MacKinnon. As she made her way out of the bush, she breathed in and caught Steve's scent mixed with diesel before it dispersed in the car's wake.

Her heart began to race and, as if to catch up with it, her body leapt into motion, galloping down the road, trying not to lose them though their speed outstripped hers. Steve was following Linc's trail, not by scent obviously, but by prearranged plan.

She tasted their dust and a cloud obscured her from their view. The air cleared as the station wagon pulled away from her. Her lungs burned with speed and dirt road. Just as she feared they would drive out of sight, the station wagon slowed and made a sharp right turn.

It disappeared. All that was left on the road was the swirling dust that danced behind. She raced through it, once again catching a faint whiff of Linc. Her lungs hurt from hard use in bad air, but she reached the dirt lane they had turned down.

Free of the worst of the dust cloud, she rediscovered Linc's trail. No wonder he had left home so long ago. He'd walked down here to meet up with Steve who was arriving by car. The idea of Steve and Linc meeting in such an out-of-the-way area filled her with dismay. What had the boy gotten himself into? He was too young and he needed her protection. She pushed herself to reach the end of the lane and as she did so, she recalled Linc's excitement when his avatar had won the last Flamequest battle.

This fight wouldn't be so easy. And it would be real.

She slowed down. Where the lane opened up into a clearing, she slipped into the bush and circled around the open area. Meanwhile the car drove straight ahead, bouncing over the uneven field. She made her roundabout way towards the small lake where Linc waited. As the car pulled up beside Linc, she wished David were here to give her courage. Steve frightened her.

Linc stood ramrod straight. Fear could do that to posture. Fear that she had smelled in his trail. His arms wrapped tightly around a white plastic rectangle she recognized as his computer.

The car stopped and two men emerged. The driver, Steve, ambled around the engine and approached Linc. Veronica's hackles rose and a low growl escaped her throat. She wanted to act now. Attack. Blood pulsed through her body. Her pack was threatened.

You need to think, too. She forced herself to observe the second man. He was middle-aged, tall and potbellied.

Linc gaped at him in recognition. "Mr. LeBlanc?"

"Hello, Linc." LeBlanc proffered his hand. Linc unwrapped his thin right arm from his computer to shake.

"I'll take that." Steve easily wrested the white laptop from Linc's one-handed grip.

"Hey," protested Linc.

Steve removed a hammer attached to his belt. He grinned

at Linc and swung it up, close enough to the boy's head that Linc cringed and retreated. "I can use this on your computer, or I can take a swing at you. Which would you prefer?"

Linc stepped back again, one foot now in the lake.

"Hand it over," ordered LeBlanc and Steve obliged. The man flipped open the laptop. "What's your password, Linc?" he asked conversationally.

"Aragorn," Linc muttered.

LeBlanc laughed. "I should have known. After all, Aragorn broke into our database, didn't he?" He stared at the screen. "Well, show me the document."

Linc stared at him.

"Yes, you." LeBlanc gestured impatiently. "I don't know who the hell else I'd be talking to."

Tentatively, Linc came to his side and pointed to something on the screen.

"Ah, Federation Bank folder. Well, that's us, isn't it?"

Linc didn't answer.

Steve nudged him with the hammer head and Linc flinched. "Yes," he said, voice high.

Veronica crept closer, now visible, but low to the ground and quiet. She wanted to be able to move quickly. These men might just play with Linc or they might decide to really hurt him. If so, they'd have to hurt her, too. Unless she ripped out their throats. At that thought, blood pounded through her body and her lip curled back.

"Did you copy this information elsewhere?" LeBlanc asked Linc.

"No."

"How do I know that's true?"

Linc's voice went higher. "I showed them my program. Not the data. I didn't want to get you in trouble. I just wanted to protect myself."

"Do you want your father to go to jail, Linc?" asked LeBlanc. "Because of your stupidity?"

"I didn't copy the data!" Linc shouted, voice tearful. "You told me not to and I didn't."

Despite hurting for Linc and his desire to protect his father, Veronica felt some guarded relief. They weren't threatening Linc with physical harm, they were threatening to incriminate his father. She thought, she *hoped*, Linc could walk away from this.

"Your uncle was interested." LeBlanc wouldn't let go of this issue. "You probably emailed it to him."

"No! He doesn't like my father."

"All the more reason."

Linc shook his head.

"You went to the police."

"I didn't tell them I saved the data. I just wanted some protection after your death threat."

"Linc, Linc, don't be melodramatic. Death threat, my goodness. I was simply explaining the gravity of the situation, that's all. But," he continued smoothly, "why not show the police the data if you were under their protection?"

"What protection? They didn't believe me. Besides, Dad said he would pay if I did." Linc's voice choked and Veronica's blood thundered. She was so close to attack. LeBlanc's white throat deserved her anger. As did Steve's. Linc was just a pup.

LeBlanc gazed at Linc for a few minutes while the boy twitched under his scrutiny. "Good boy." Then he clapped Linc on the back and Linc shuddered. "You know, if we find out you're lying to us, your father *will* pay."

"I know, Mr. LeBlanc," said Linc in a low eager voice.

"Here." LeBlanc tossed the computer to Steve. It landed at his feet.

"No!" cried Linc as Steve lifted the hammer and swung it in an arc, smashing down on the white plastic. More than once. Linc's shoulders sagged and Veronica heard him sniffle as he stood there, mesmerized by the hammer's actions.

"My stuff was on that." Linc sounded inconsolable. She thought of all the time and love he had spent on his role-playing game.

"Throw it in the water for good measure." As LeBlanc ambled towards the station wagon, Veronica heard a second car driving along the dirt lane that led to this lake. Neither of the two men or Linc were aware they had company. It wasn't till after the laptop sank into the water, that Steve, walking towards the car, froze.

"Someone's here," Steve told LeBlanc. The men stared at each other for a long moment, then looked at Linc who hadn't moved away from the lake that held his computer. LeBlanc nodded. Steve's body tensed and his hand went to his side. In that moment, everything had changed.

Veronica wanted to yell, *Run, Linc, run.* But all she could do was bark furiously and race towards him.

Her surprise appearance bought them a few seconds. While LeBlanc slid into the station wagon and started the engine, Steve stopped and stared, as if she were an apparition. Then his knife was in his hand and he was running towards Linc. Steve wanted him as hostage.

At the last minute Linc recognized his new danger and began to race towards Veronica. She pushed up her speed and reached Linc just before Steve did. Snarling and growling, she leapt between Linc and the knife. Steve braced for her attack.

Her mind went numb, though the wolf's body did not. It watched the man's movements carefully. She'd been here before. That much she knew, though the details were different. Her body had been different, too. More vulnerable. *Human.* She'd faced this man with a knife and lost. This encounter he wasn't going to hurt her. She was wolf and too strong.

"Call your dog off or I'll kill it," yelled Steve at Linc.

Linc stopped and turned. "Goldie, run," he shouted.

No. She would not run again. Though she willed Linc to do just that.

But Steve had the human voice and he said, "Get over here, Linc. *Now.*"

Linc slumped and to her utter dismay he bravely began to walk towards them, all for a wolf he barely knew.

In his victory, Steve took his eyes off her for a moment. Veronica jumped at the knife hand. He moved just before she reached him, but it wasn't soon enough. Her teeth clamped down on the vulnerable wrist and, tasting blood, she tore skin and tendon.

Screaming, Steve dropped the knife. She released him and went for his source of power, the knife. He stumbled back from her, his free hand gripping his wrist while blood ran down his arm. Her wolf-self was unrepentant. He was lucky she hadn't gone for his throat while defending her pack. Because she wanted to destroy this threat.

The station wagon drove away from them. Steve was left behind, screaming, crouched over his damaged limb. But LeBlanc wouldn't get far. A police car sat on the top of the lane, blocking his way out.

"Goldie?" asked Linc over the painful noise of Steve keening. "Are you okay?"

Veronica trotted over and dropped the knife at Linc's feet. She had to get out of here before the police decided she was dangerous enough to shoot. She licked Linc's hand once in reassurance, and ran.

ℴ

David was lightheaded with relief. Not ideal, given he was driving. But the police had just phoned his cell to say they'd found Linc and Linc was safe. David blinked back tears as he gripped the steering wheel tightly, and made himself focus on the driving. No sense losing it now. Especially on this gravel road.

He turned onto the dirt lane that led to Carey Lake. He'd been here a few times in the past with high-school girlfriends, but not much since. Apparently, Carey Lake had become a meeting place for reasons other than necking with your latest crush. He wished that was all Linc had ever thought to do here. To think Nell had been pleased Linc wasn't yet interested in girls. At the moment, David was convinced that where Linc was concerned any interest outside of computers would be a good thing.

He realized a man was screaming. A man, not a boy. They'd said Linc was fine, safe, unharmed. David gunned the engine and the car bounced over the uneven road while the anguished noise continued to unnerve David. He had to reach the clearing and see what the hell was going on.

The screaming faded as he caught sight of Linc jogging towards him. The boy was in one piece, thank God. David slammed on the brakes and jumped out, scanning the area to see a police car with a man locked in the back, an empty station wagon and two officers hovering over some guy in pain.

Steve MacKinnon.

"Uncle David!" Linc exclaimed. David strode forward and grabbed his nephew's shoulders, alternately shaking and hugging him. It took quite a while before he could speak and to make up for it he banged Linc's back a few times.

"I'd kill you if I hadn't been so worried," he finally managed.

Linc snorted at this declaration of affection and David hugged him again. When he stepped back, he saw that the boy, strangely, held a knife. He stared in consternation. At least it wasn't bloody. Presumably Linc hadn't used it on anyone.

"Uh, Linc, what the hell are you doing with that?"

Linc looked down, as if just remembering. "Goldie gave it to me."

"*Goldie?*" David rocked back on his feet. While he knew Veronica had planned to track Linc, he hadn't actually thought it possible.

"Yeah." Linc misunderstood David's incredulous expression. "I couldn't believe it either."

"She was here?"

"It was her, Uncle David. I know it was. She saved my life by disarming Steve. And then she licked my hand." From Linc's delivery, it wasn't clear which of these two events was more important.

Disarmed Steve? "Is Goldie okay?"

Linc bobbed his head enthusiastically. "She ran off though. You won't see her now. But anyway what happened was that Steve guy smashed my computer and then he pulled a knife on me, like he did on you the other night. Then Goldie appeared out of nowhere. It was like she just materialized, you know? Whoosh, she was there protecting me. Can you believe it? I didn't think she liked me all that much."

"Is Goldie all right?"

Linc looked at David. "Yeah, she was all right. She ran off," he added slowly, as if hoping this time the information would sink in. "So anyway, she's between Steve MacKinnon and me and then he says he's going to hurt her"—Linc held up a hand, clearly aware this was a point on which David needed reassurance—"*but he didn't.* She bit his arm and ripped it open. He dropped the knife and the only one bleeding was him. He's been screaming and crying ever since. It's kinda gross."

David felt his mouth open and shut.

"Oh, then she brought me the knife and ran away. Weird, eh?"

"Pretty weird." David felt incapable of saying anything more intelligible. Concern for Veronica now warred with relief for Linc. She'd been frightened of Steve and forced to confront him. Obviously she'd bested him. He decided that since Goldie was, according to Linc, safe, to focus on Linc, his overexcited, somewhat shaken nephew.

"So, Linc, what exactly are you doing here at Carey Lake?"

For the first time, Linc looked as if he might have done something wrong. "They were going to put my father in jail if I didn't bring them my computer."

"They?"

"The bank. LeBlanc, specifically."

"Your dad's boss."

Linc nodded.

"How could LeBlanc put Aaron in jail?"

"Well." Linc cleared his throat. "Dad turned a blind eye to the money laundering, which was kind of bad since he's the forensic accountant."

"Why didn't you tell me this earlier?"

Linc scuffed his foot. "I wanted to, but Dad had a fit when I suggested it."

David swore. He could imagine Aaron had received a tidy sum to do his job badly.

Linc's face became animated. "That's why he wouldn't look at my idea about my zip program. He didn't want me to find out about the laundering. Not because he didn't think my program was a good idea." Linc jabbed a finger in the air to emphasize this point. "Dad *knew* it was a good idea."

David just shook his head. He didn't say more because an officer was approaching them.

"Chris Evans." The tall, red-haired man clapped Linc on the shoulder. "Are you okay?"

"I guess. It was kinda scary."

"Yes, it was. Good thing your dog was around to save you."

Linc nodded dumbly.

"Well, we'll have to ask you some questions. Can you follow us back to the station?"

"Yes," said David. "But I'd like to pick up his mother on the way."

"Sure." The officer relieved Linc of his knife. "Your dog knew how to disarm a man. Has it been trained?"

"I don't know," Linc muttered.

"Well, you got off lucky. Steve MacKinnon is known to be fond of knives."

"He said he would hurt Goldie."

"Well, he was wrong, wasn't he? Goldie hurt him and good for her." With a smile, Evans turned away.

Another cruiser arrived, David wasn't sure what they were doing, but he and Linc went to retrieve his battered computer out of the lake. It didn't take long for Linc to wade in and find it. David whistled at the dripping, mangled plastic and metal. At Linc's misery, he added, "I'm sorry, though worse things can be broken, you know. Your bones. Goldie."

"Yeah." Linc still looked pretty sad.

"That was brave of you to protect your father. Misguided, but brave. I could kill Aaron myself now."

"It wouldn't have happened if I hadn't stolen Dad's password."

"Did Aaron point that out to you?"

Linc shrugged.

"It also wouldn't have happened if they hadn't broken the law."

"Yeah, well."

"Let's get going. We need to tell your mother."

Linc let out a long sigh. Then he brightened visibly. "Do you think that Goldie will visit us once in a while, now that she's found us again?"

"I don't know that she's found us anywhere but at Carey Lake."

"Oh."

"Besides," said David grimly. "If people discover that a wild wolf bit someone, they might not want her around."

"She was protecting me!"

"We know that. Not everyone will believe it." Despite Linc's eagerness to see Goldie again, David needed to tell Veronica to keep a low profile.

Chapter Fourteen

David and Linc found Nell at work treating an elderly cat. She took one look at Linc, ordered them to the backroom and joined them in less than five minutes.

"Okay," she demanded, hands on hips. "What happened *now*?"

David supposed they might look like two delinquents, but they were actually nephew and uncle. He let Linc respond, but when his explanation stuttered to a stop, David stepped into the breach.

"You *idiot!*" Nell declared halfway through and hugged Linc fiercely. Not long after, Nell shut down her clinic and the three of them set off for the police station.

David stayed as long as required, two hours in total. By that time, he had satisfied the police with his side of the story and he had learned enough about Steve MacKinnon to be thoroughly alarmed for Veronica. He left and, ignoring speed limits, raced down Main Street towards Nell's house.

He wanted Veronica gone and he wanted her gone now. Though Steve had been weakened by Veronica's attack, he'd been loquacious enough to tell the police about the existence of Veronica. They weren't too impressed David had hid her from them. In fact, they disapproved. She might be a missing person and with her amnesia, she needed medical help.

David had managed to act like these things had never occurred to him while Linc had been boggled Veronica was an amnesiac, *just like* The Bourne Identity!

"What happened to her ex-husband?" he asked while David hushed him.

So, in the police's eyes, David was no longer the good uncle looking after Linc, or not just that. He was also the idiot asshole who didn't know enough to help vulnerable women.

He was just grateful the police showed minimal interest in Steve's assertions that Veronica had a well-trained pet wolf who wanted to kill him, and that he was well-connected with the FBI. But David couldn't count on the latter being bogus. If the FBI had some inkling about werewolves and Veronica, she could be in deep trouble. His tires screeched as he took the corner too fast. Nell's street came into view. He didn't bother with the stop sign and peeled into the driveway. To his relief, no strange vehicles were parked nearby.

The street was quiet. But Steve had told police the FBI were on their way to find Veronica—he'd phoned them after his little visit last night.

David flung open the door. "Veronica!" he bellowed.

"Hey." She emerged from the kitchen, all smiles at the sight of him.

He strode towards her. "Are you okay?"

"Yes. How is Linc?"

He pulled her to him and held tight, as if that would convey everything he had to tell her.

"David?" she asked in confusion.

He let go. "You have to get out of here. Steve has been talking about you, to the police, to the FBI. He says someone wants to find you. He might be talking up his ass, but we need to play it safe."

"What does the FBI want with me?"

"I don't know. He also told the police you're amnesiac and have a pet wolf."

She paled.

"He doesn't know you *are* a wolf and the police aren't interested in the wolf. But he does claim the FBI paid him to inform on you. He thinks this will impress the guys arresting him."

She looked panicked. "The FBI might know more about me than Steve."

"My fear exactly."

"Do you know when they're coming?"

"Any time, according to Steve, which might mean now, which might mean never. But we can't take chances here. You need to leave." He kissed her quick and hard. Held her face in his hands. "Veronica, go."

"I don't want to leave you." She sounded forlorn.

"Listen, we can meet again."

"Thank you."

"Don't thank me," he said, exasperated. "I *want* to see you again."

She smiled and kissed his cheek. "I'll come to your place in Peterborough."

"Good. I'll give you money."

"I don't want your money and I can't carry it anyway. It's best if Veronica disappears."

His hands dropped away. He was worried he'd never see her again. "How many days to travel?"

"Maybe a week. I checked it out on a map once," she

explained, slightly sheepish, as if embarrassed she'd planned to travel to Peterborough.

"I'll be there," he assured her. "Now that Linc is finally safe." It was a relief to only have one person to fear for. He recited his address and phone number.

"I already know it," she said quietly.

They stood there, not quite touching. He knuckled her cheek briefly, unwilling to do more in that moment. She had to get moving.

Her gaze intensified. "I'll see you there. I promise."

Then she was gone and the place was empty. Mindlessly, David roamed the house, then stared out the windows as if that would let him know where Veronica was and what she was doing. He hoped she put many miles between them. Eventually he gave up looking into the night and wandered the house again, still at loose ends, unable to solve the problem and the mystery of Veronica. Because he understood so little about her, he worried when she was wolf.

An hour later, Linc and Nell came home, and his mother insisted on a visit, too.

David was wiped out by the day's events, but Linc was pumped high. He had saved his father from jail, helped in the arrest of money-launderer Henry LeBlanc and been briefly reunited with his favorite wolf, Goldie.

"See, Gran, she *is* a good wolf. And you had your doubts when we came back from the camping trip. You thought we'd been with a dangerous animal."

"Well, she could have been dangerous," David's mother pointed out.

"No. If you met her, you'd know she was gentle. Except with guys like Steve MacKinnon."

At the mention of the man who had pulled a knife on her grandson, her face softened. "It seems quite amazing to me but," she added when Linc began to protest again, "since this Goldie protected you, I'll agree she is a good wolf."

Linc sat back, satisfied. "Even the police agreed." Then Linc's face fell a little. "I wish we knew where Veronica was so we could help her." He looked accusingly at David. "Why didn't you tell me she'd lost her memory?"

"Well..." It was beyond David to explain.

His mother jumped to his defense. "He probably thought Veronica was lying, Linc."

"Mom, no," said David.

"Some people are con artists, you know," she continued as if he hadn't spoken.

"Not Veronica," claimed loyal Linc. "She's a good person."

Nell came to David's rescue. "All right, despite all these good wolves and people, I'm *exhausted*. Let's head to bed, shall we? We can talk in the morning."

The three of them trudged around the house, saying good night to Eleanor as she left, then getting ready for bed, which took some effort on Linc's part. He was overexcited.

And so was David, or overtired. In any event, he lay down and could not sleep. Thoughts ran through his head and he felt as if something physical propped open his eyelids. He waited, perhaps for sleep, perhaps for night visitors in search of Veronica. No one came and just before the sky began to lighten at dawn, David dozed.

At seven o'clock in the morning a car pulled into the driveway. The sound of the engine entered his dreams—it was Steve's station wagon bearing down on an injured Veronica and David hadn't time to save her. Then David awoke, sweating in fear and sitting up. The engine switched off and two car doors slammed shut. He registered that it was daylight. Nell was up. Someone knocked.

David bounded out of bed and down the stairs. Nell, already at the door, had a politely inquiring expression on her face.

"Hello?" She shifted on her feet, in what David recognized as nervousness. He would have preferred she hadn't opened the door and he suspected she now felt the same. After Steve, everyone was wary of unexpected and unwelcome visitors.

"Good morning, ma'am," said someone with a strong American accent.

David came to stand beside her, observing two men through the screen. The second, younger man hung back.

"I'm sorry to disturb you so early in the morning," the first man continued politely, as if he were selling Nell something.

His manner and the American accent threw Nell off and she looked confused.

"Can I help you?" She frowned as the man, tall, broad, and all muscle, flashed a badge.

"I'm an FBI agent—"

"FBI?" said Nell.

"Yes, from the Federal—"

"FBI?" she exclaimed more loudly. A distinctly hysterical tone entered her voice. She looked at David in alarm. "My God, *what has Linc done now?*"

David could just see the gears whirring in his sister's head, coming up with new hacking scenarios that involved the national security of the United States.

"I'm not here about anyone called the Linc," put in the man quickly.

"Thank *God.*" Nell slumped in relief. "As a mother, there is only so much I can take in one week."

David patted her shoulder.

"I'm Special Agent Walters." He opened his mouth to continue but stopped as the second man stepped forward. David had the odd impression this new guy was both sniffing and breathing through his mouth.

"She's been here." His voice was flat and showed little emotion. An odd contrast to the unshed tears that added a bright sheen to his weirdly blue eyes.

"Are you sure?" The agent ignored Nell and David, waiting on his companion's answer.

The other breathed in again. "Yes," he declared with intense, repressed joy. His entire body vibrated in a way that David found unsettling, yet oddly familiar. "Veronica. Veronica!"

The agent turned to Nell. "When was Veronica Kolski last here?"

"Veronica?" Nell, baffled by the purpose of this visit, turned to David, as did Special Agent Walters.

David shrugged. "I know a Veronica Smith." Inwardly, he winced at grabbing the most common surname he could think of. At least he hadn't said Veronica Doe. Or Veronica Wolfe.

"Smith?" repeated the agent. "Fine. When did you last see Veronica Smith?"

To David's dismay, the younger, slighter man called for Veronica again. His voice echoed through the suburb and the forest and into the morning's light.

But she was far, far away David reminded himself.

"Sir?" demanded the agent sharply and David found himself locked into the gaze of someone with pale, angry eyes.

"Yesterday, I guess." Nell was getting impatient with David's silence. "At least, *I* saw her yesterday. Did she disappear again?"

"Disappear?" repeated the agent.

Nell gave a helpless shrug. "Veronica kind of comes and goes."

The agent turned to David, pinning him with his intense gaze.

"She's gone," said David flatly. "I don't know where she is."

ℬ

When she left David last night, Veronica had planned to flee. His fear for her had driven her into the woods, had even driven her to try to shift. But her body resisted the second shift in twenty-four hours and she had to stop and think about what she was doing.

Because she had run as wolf for too long. If there was an alternative, she wanted to find it. Overnight, she developed the idea of taking a measure of the people who searched for her. Then she could better avoid them in the future. Or at least understand their motives. She understood so little of the world as it was and, to date, her unthinking, running existence had not served her well. Only luck had led her to David.

So she decided to spend the night in the woods, not far from Nell's, careful to position herself downwind. Not that her scent didn't linger in the house, but she liked the precaution nevertheless.

She dozed through the night and woke as the sun was rising, somewhat surprised to find her human self sleeping outdoors. The summer night had cooled her sufficiently that she shivered, but the temperature was not unbearable. She toyed with returning to the house and decided that was stupid. She needed to wait out the day, at the very least.

Wrapping her arms around her legs, she laid her head on her knees and dozed again, before being brought abruptly alert by a car that turned onto Nell's road and drew into Nell's driveway. She breathed in, waiting for the wind to carry their scents to her. She was too far away to see the men clearly. The breeze took its time but when their scents arrived, recognition jolted her. She could barely think for a moment, the intimately familiar smell shocked her so. She was reminded of...herself. But the scent was male, and not quite her. She began to shake with fear and anticipation. And hope.

Be careful. Steve MacKinnon and his knife had also been familiar. These men could intend her harm even if they did not trigger a danger warning as Steve had done.

It was a glimpse of her mysterious past and she had to investigate. Because these two men who now stood at Nell's front door were werewolves.

She couldn't remember meeting a werewolf before, but she was drawn inexorably towards them. Then she heard her name, echoing in the empty, early morning, called with longing and excitement by a voice she should know. She ran.

They were inside the house now, the two shapeshifters, near the front door, and she slipped in the back. A familiar voice was demanding that David stop hiding her, that they meant her no harm, that they were family.

It was the voice of her brother, for so long her one link to the past, though she'd only met him in her dreams and nightmares. She could no more avoid him, than avoid breathing. Padding silently into the house, she knew he would sense her arrival. She waited a moment, to mentally prepare herself for the encounter, and stepped into the living room.

David whirled around, astonished and dismayed. "What are you doing here?" he asked, his tone anguished. "Why did you come back?"

Her voice clogged with emotion and she cast him a look of apology before meeting the gaze of the one she knew. The sucker punch of recognition almost brought her to her knees. She shivered with sensation. This was an adult version of the boy-brother who haunted her dreams. They stared, brother-sister, strange and familiar. Years had passed and she didn't know what had happened at the beginning of that interval of time, except that she had lost everything.

"You gave me my name," she said wonderingly. "When I could remember nothing else." At one point she'd feared that, out of despair and loneliness, she had made her brother up.

He frowned as David went to stand beside her and briefly his gaze fell on David. "We aren't going to hurt her. She's my sister."

David looked at her for confirmation and she nodded, though her whole body was shaking. She closed her eyes, trying to take it all in and then she was wrapped in her brother's arms, his damp face on her hair. He smelled like her, he smelled like home.

"I thought you were dead," he choked out.

She didn't even know his name. "What do I call you?" she asked into his shoulder.

He pulled back, hands on her arms now, as if he couldn't believe that she was real. "Seth. Do you not know me?"

"Seth." She tried out the syllable. It felt right. It matched his beautiful eyes, his dark face. She raised a hand to his cheek. "I've lost my memory."

He frowned, unsure of what she meant. "Did you"—he dropped his voice to a bare murmur so David and Nell couldn't hear—"go feral?" He was referring to her constant wolf state.

"Yes. Because I remembered nothing at all. *Nothing.*"

"Yet you recognize me?"

"From my dreams." She smiled a little. "It was as if you used to visit me."

They stared while he took this information in.

She shook her head in disbelief. "I was always so worried about you in my dreams. I'm not sure why."

He smiled back, though it was bittersweet. "Because you're my older sister and growing up you always protected me."

She was quite struck by this window on her past. She rather liked this information about herself. "Really? How old am I now?"

"Twenty-seven. You've been gone three years."

She glanced around. Nell had tactfully slipped back upstairs. Linc had never come down. It was safe to talk frankly. "I've been wolf for quite a long time then."

David glanced at the other man in alarm. He, in turn, became even more expressionless and for the first time Veronica became aware of the man who had accompanied her brother here. She wished Seth had come alone. The other was not familiar.

"He's a werewolf, too, David," she said softly, eying Seth's companion.

David looked incredulous. "You're a werewolf *and* an FBI agent?"

"That's right. Trey Walters." He extended his hand and Veronica reluctantly shook it. "You're my niece. I've been helping Seth with his search, since I have a few extra resources."

"Oh." Trey did have Seth's eyes.

"We haven't actually met before today, so you wouldn't remember me if you could," he explained.

"Oh." She had the feeling she would be saying *oh* a lot in the next few days. The four of them stared at each other.

David's relief was palpable and he spoke first, clearing his throat. "I'm glad for you, Veronica. You've found your family."

"We don't usually tell people we're werewolves," Seth quietly told his sister.

"David is safe," she assured Seth. "He's been very good to me. He took me in when no one else would have."

Seth turned to David. "Thank you. You've been generous." His manner was stiff. "From now on we can take care of Veronica."

David's face became harsh, mask-like. "If that's what she wants."

She wanted to spend time with Seth and possibly her uncle, get to know her family, her kind. But the thought of leaving David hurt.

"I want to be with you," she told David. Seth moved closer as if to protect her from an interloper, something David could never be. She would have to explain just how important David was to her. His sky blue eyes were hard now and she wasn't sure why.

"You should sort out what has happened to you. Get reacquainted with Seth. After, you can visit me in Peterborough." For a brief moment, David's expression was wistful. "Like we planned."

He grabbed her hand, his grip strong and sure. Then he released her and stepped back. "You'd better go, before the local police become too interested. They consider you a matter of some concern. I'm a terrible liar, but I can say you left early this morning and I don't know where you've gone. But..." he faltered and his expression softened.

She tilted her head in question.

"If you want," he repeated, "come see me."

℃

David picked up the phone. "Hello?" After four weeks of radio silence, he was still embarrassingly eager to talk to Veronica. And she never called. Maybe she didn't want to hear shit like, *Come back, I miss you,* or worse, *I've never felt this way about a lover.* He wasn't even sure he could say those words, they were locked so tightly in his chest.

"Hi, David," said Nell. He shut his eyes and wiped the sweat from his forehead. "How are you?"

It was a humid night and he didn't have air conditioning. "Hot."

"Yeah, well, August, you know."

"How's Linc?"

"Good. He's reading *Lord of the Rings* and he likes it."

"It's about time, given all he's done in the name of Aragorn."

She laughed. "I know."

"So, he's surviving without a computer?"

"Yes. Still a bit obsessive, but books aren't quite such an alarming obsession."

"Can't hack through books."

"Too true." She paused. "We're getting a dog. Husky. So he'll stop talking about the damn wolf that saved his life."

"She's a good wolf."

"Oh, believe me, I know she's good, David. How could I not, living with Linc?"

"A dog sounds like an excellent idea."

"I hope so." She paused and David braced himself for Nell's next question. "Have you heard from Veronica?"

"No." He wanted to get off the phone now.

"I'm sorry."

"Don't be."

"I was even beginning to like her. She should at least call and let you know how she is. Did she give you a number?"

"It all happened too quickly," he defended Veronica. Though he didn't know why she didn't phone. Or he did and he wasn't ready to admit she had moved on, now that she didn't need him so desperately. Of course she'd be more comfortable with other werewolves. "How's Aaron?"

"His lawyer says he'll get off with community service."

The doorbell rang.

"Someone there?"

"I guess." He wandered towards the door, expecting a neighbor, then stopped moving, frozen.

Veronica stood outside, framed by the screen, slightly blurred by its fine mesh.

He just stared. Her golden eyes shone and she shifted under his gaze, as if nervous. She smiled tentatively.

"David?" said Nell.

"Uh." He smiled back, laughing a little. He was incredibly pleased to see her.

"David. Answer me," snapped Nell.

He waved Veronica in. He found it hard to speak past the lump in his throat. "Nell, got to go," he forced out.

"You sound funny. Who's there?"

"Veronica," he admitted though he wanted to keep this reunion private. Special.

"Good, I'll say goodbye then."

They hung up.

He cleared his throat as he turned to focus completely on Veronica. "I thought you might phone me."

She ducked her head. "I should have. I'm sorry."

"I was worried. I thought I rated a call." He winced because he didn't want to sound whiney. But he'd feared he would never know what happened to her and that had bothered him greatly.

"You did rate a call. I picked up the phone a few times, but I chickened out. I thought it would be easier to say what I have to say in person."

His stomach dropped out the bottom. Till now, he hadn't realized how much he was counting on a future with Veronica. Her absence, though not reassuring, had been filled with possibility when he looked at it sideways. Now she was going to end that.

"I would have come sooner but Seth didn't want me to travel under the full moon. It can be dangerous if you don't have good control." She glanced at him to see his reaction.

"I see," he said lamely.

"It's all been pretty weird."

He rubbed the back of his neck. "I guess." He couldn't see where she was going with this.

Then she spoke in a rush. "Three years ago my then-boyfriend gave me a severe concussion. Seth believes that caused the amnesia. In fact, if I'd been a normal human I probably wouldn't have survived. My shifting saved me, even if it lost me my mind."

"Oh, Veronica." *Three years.*

"Seth never liked him," she hurried on. "Said I deliberately chose unsuitable men all the time, but this one was the worst, the most violent and the one I kept returning to."

He wanted to say, *I'm not like that. I would never hurt you.* But if she didn't know now, he wasn't sure how to convince her before she left for good.

"Did you see him again, this boyfriend?" he asked, his voice strained.

"He's dead. Seth killed him in self-defense."

David let out a whistle.

"You can't tell anyone that." Her eyes were dark, almost bruised, and he wanted to take her into his arms. But she held herself stiffly, arms crossed, as if to prevent contact.

"I won't," was all he said.

"You can't tell anyone that Seth and I are werewolves."

He smiled crookedly. "For a while now I've understood this information isn't for general consumption."

She nodded. "I know but Seth is nervous about you. I promised him I'd make this clear to you, even though I personally didn't think it necessary."

"Did Seth want you to see me again?"

She looked around guiltily which puzzled David. "Oh, he knew I had to come."

David frowned. "He did?" Was that understanding on her brother's part, or enthusiasm for a clean break?

"Though he's glad you're different from the men I was with before. Not that I remember them."

He eyed her. "I'm not sure what you're saying."

"I've missed you, David. A lot. But." She stood straighter, as if she needed to deliver a speech. "Don't feel obligated, okay? I have a family now—I'm an aunt with an adorable niece and nephew!—who can look after me. Seth got me ID."

"Great. I'm glad you're doing fine." That hearty tone of his. He hated it.

She winced. "I didn't know how to say this on the phone. I'm not supposed to say it all at once. I should have tea or something—except it's too hot—and chat about what we've been doing..." She wrung her hands. "I don't know how to say this," she finished hopelessly and strangely enough, David felt hope.

"Veronica." He put two hands on her arms and rubbed them up and down, thinking to derail her Dear John speech. "I'm glad you're here. I've missed you."

She kept talking. "It won't work if you don't care for me, too. Beyond obligation-type caring, that is."

"What?" He couldn't make sense of her words though she was speaking English. She wouldn't meet his gaze.

"It can't just be me who wants you," she continued, as if putting her heart on the line and finally David had the sense that she was not saying goodbye. "Not in the long run. It will gut me if you don't love me back."

"Veronica!" He placed a thumb on her cheekbone, a palm on her lovely face. His heart rose. "I told you. I wanted you to come back."

"Well, not exactly. You told me to come back, if I want."

"Same thing." He kissed her, briefly, intensely.

"No, it's not," she said a little indignant.

"I want you," he declared, in case that wasn't clear.

She looked at him warily. He might have to work up to saying he loved her. It was true, but he found the words difficult to say aloud.

"How do you feel about commitment?" she asked.

"It's a good concept."

"Concept?"

He winced. "I want to be committed to you, that is, *I am*," he admitted. He trailed a hand up her arm and she shivered under his touch.

"Good," she said with clear relief.

He pulled her into his arms and she curled into him.

"I've chosen you as my mate," she blurted into his neck.

He pulled back to look at her. "Mate?"

"We like to mate for life, us wolves, though relationships do break and we can mate again if one of us dies. Or so Seth tells me. This is why it took all my courage to come see you. I worry that you pity me and want to protect me, but that's it. Well, and perhaps some lust." Her smile was wry.

"There might be *some* lust."

She smacked his chest. "This is serious." But her expression had lightened.

"It is certainly not pity." He felt vast relief she'd come back to him *for him*, that he hadn't simply been a safe place until she found her brother.

"So, what do you think?"

He kissed her beautiful mouth. "I choose *you* as *my* mate."

About the Author

Jorrie Spencer has written for more years than she can remember. Her latest writing passion is romance and werewolves. She lives with her husband and two children in Canada and is thrilled to be published with Samhain.

To learn more about Jorrie Spencer please visit www.jorriespencer.com. Send an email to Jorrie Spencer at jorriespencer@gmail.com or join her Yahoo! group http://groups.yahoo.com/group/jorriespencer.

She also writes as Joely Skye (www.joelyskye.com).

How much trouble can one small female be to a modern-day shapeshifting Viking? Well...it really depends on local gun laws.

Go Fetch
© 2007 Shelly Laurenston

Conall Víga-Feilan, direct descendent of Viking shifters, never thought he'd meet a female strong enough to be his mate. He especially didn't think a short, viper-tongued human would ever fit the bill. But Miki Kendrick isn't some average human. With an IQ off the charts and a special skill with weapons of all kinds, Miki brings the big blond pooch to his knees—and keeps him there.

Miki's way too smart to ever believe in love and she knows a guy like Conall could only want one thing from her. But with the Pack's enemies on her tail and a few days stuck alone with the one man who makes her absolutely wild, Miki is about to discover how persistent one Viking wolf can be.

Available now in ebook from Samhain Publishing.

Enjoy the following excerpt from Go Fetch...

"Hey, Miki." He didn't look up, simply kept untying her laces. And, even though he couldn't see the fronts of her boots, was probably taking a lot longer than actually necessary.

"Hey, Conall."

"How's it going? You have a good trip?"

Miki had to swallow to get the words out. "Yeah." Okay. One word. Apparently she couldn't manage any better at the moment. All the guy was doing was helping her off with her boots. Of course, he was on his knees doing it. She kind of liked him on his knees.

Get a grip, Kendrick.

She needed to start talking. Now. "How's it going with you?"

He still didn't look up; instead, watching his own big hands slowly remove one boot then start on the other. His hair, thick and almost white blond, fell in front of his face. Like hers, it was longer than when she last saw him, just brushing across his shoulders. His hair reminded her of silk and she wondered if it would feel that way against her skin.

"Pretty good," he murmured softly.

He slid the other boot off and placed it aside. Leaning back on his haunches, he ran his hands over her calves and feet while staring at her face. He had the lightest blue eyes she'd ever seen and they completely mesmerized her.

"Anything else you need help taking off?" he asked gruffly.

Miki almost said "everything" but caught herself. She pulled her feet away from Conall's wonderful touch and pulled herself up to her knees. Smirking, she gave a little wave. "No. I'm fine. But thanks." He slowly stood, his eyes never leaving her face. Still on her knees, she moved back away from him as his body kept rising. She'd forgotten exactly how tall he was. And exactly how big. In some respects, the man *was* a bear.

So busy staring and trying to stay away from him, Miki fell right off the bed.

"Miki?" She looked up to find him on the bed, hovering over her. "Are you okay?" He didn't even try to stifle his laughter. Great. Now he could see exactly the level of her geekiness. It was off the charts, she knew. Well, that should convince him she was definitely not the woman for him. A guy like Conall should get some vacuous super-model babe who couldn't complete a full sentence or even spell sentence.

"I'm fine." She sat up, but before she could struggle to her feet, Conall moved around the bed to stand behind her. His big hands slid under her arms and lifted her off the floor as if she weighed no more than a bag of chips.

"Uh...thanks," she bit out as her feet touched solid ground. She tried to pull away from him, but he wasn't letting her go. Instead, he pulled her back until he held her against his chest. His arms slid around her body and he leaned in close, gently trapping her arms against her sides. If this were anybody else, she would have completely flipped out. They'd be lucky if they had their eyes when she was done. But she couldn't even concentrate when Conall had his hands on her.

Husky, against her ear, "I missed you, Mik."

The man was killing her. "Conall?"

"Miki?" He nuzzled her neck as one of his—*huge!*—hands slid over her breast. Immediately her nipples hardened. She blinked. *When the hell did that start happening?*

"I think you need to back off." At least she was pretty sure she said that. She was having trouble concentrating. Especially with his tongue sliding up across her neck to her ear.

"You *think*?" His hand squeezed her breast and her back arched. "Or you *know*?"

Oh boy, he's good. Miki bet that with very little effort, Conall could turn a nun into a whore. Of course, she wasn't a nun.

She yanked her body away from his and it was as if her skin started to yell at the loss of him.

Miki backed away. "Conall. Don't get the wrong idea."

"And what idea is that?"

"I'm not going to sleep with you."

He took a step towards her. "I am so not talking about sleeping."

She backed up again. "You're not going to make this easy on me, are you, Viking?"

He took another step forward. "Not on your life, Kendrick."

She backed up once again and slammed into a dresser. She held her arm up as if to ward him off. "Stay!"

And he did.

"Look, you're an unnaturally large, good-looking guy. I'm sure there are a plethora of women out there who would be perfect for you."

"Personally, I like women who can successfully use 'plethora' in a sentence."

Dammit, the bastard made her smile. She hated that. Especially when he smiled back. He was truly gorgeous. And as dangerous as they come.

Forcing her smile under control, "I'm going to take a shower. So you need to piss off." She walked to the bathroom and as she stepped into the luxurious and huge room, she realized Conall stood behind her. Okay. Now this was just getting creepy.

She turned around. "Is there something else?"

"No. Not at all."

"Okay. Well, I'm going to take a shower...by myself."

"Great." They stared at each other. She couldn't understand what the fuck he was grinning at. Then, finally, with a low chuckle he asked, "You do know this is my bathroom?"

Miki closed her eyes. "What?"

"Yeah. In fact, this is *my* room."

She gritted her teeth. Great. That wonderful smell on the neatly made bed had been Conall. And who the fuck made their bed these days anyway? Miki didn't make her bed unless she was changing the sheets.

"She told me it was the second door on the right."

"Actually, yours is third. Right next door."

"Of course it is." She would *kill* Sara.

"But, please, feel free to stay. Take all the showers you want. I can help with the soap."

Images of that danced through her besotted brain and it felt as if someone squeezed her lungs because she was having a lot of trouble breathing.

"Well, that's very neighborly of you, Viking. But I'll just go to my own room."

He wasn't completely blocking her way, but she had to slide against him to get out of the bathroom and she felt that connection all the way down to her toes. She almost moaned.

"Well, see you at dinner," she squeaked out.

Then she ran.

GET IT NOW

MyBookStoreAndMore.com
GREAT EBOOKS, GREAT DEALS . . . AND MORE!

Don't wait to run to the bookstore down the street, or waste time shopping online at one of the "big boys." Now, all your favorite Samhain authors are all in one place—at MyBookStoreAndMore.com. Stop by today and discover great deals on Samhain—and a whole lot more!

 Samhain Publishing ltd

WWW.SAMHAINPUBLISHING.COM

hot stuff

Discover Samhain!

THE HOTTEST NEW PUBLISHER ON THE PLANET

Romance, fantasy, mystery, thriller, mainstream and
more—Samhain has more selection, hotter authors, and
everything's available in both ebook and print.

Pick your favorite, sit back, and enjoy the ride!
Hot stuff indeed.

WWW.SAMHAINPUBLISHING.COM